DANNY AND HIS GRANDFATHERS

UNITED CREATURES UNIVERSE STORIES

RANDALL FOX

OAKE FOX PUBLISHING

CONTENT AND
TRIGGER WARNINGS

This story mentions child abuse, sexual assault, suicidal ideation/assisted suicide, attempted murder, and parental/grandparental death.

This story contains or references profanity, terminal illnesses, smoking, grief/young-child mourning, physical violence, dyslexia/learning-disability discrimination, and past miscarriage.

Even with a young protagonist and a part-time narrator, this story is not targeted at or considered young adult or children's fiction and deals with adult topics.

ARTIFICIAL INTELLIGENCE DISCLAIMER

Grammarly was used to aid with spelling, punctuation, grammar, and word order.

Artificial intelligence was used to aid in generating the Content and Trigger Warning statement text.

Other than as mentioned above, no generative AI tools were used to create the text of this work of fiction.

CHAPTER 1

like it when spring comes to our Earthside house in New Chicago. Daddy jokes that spring in New Chicago is two weeks between winter and summer, and that they come a day at a time over several months. I don't know if that is true. I've never spent a whole spring there. We always head to space in April.

Six months in space and six months Earthside. That is how I've lived my life since I was tiny. Mommy says I went into space when I was only a few weeks old.

I share my birthday with Uncle Mark, who is my favorite creature in the entire world, on March 16. He's called me his 24th birthday present and his best birthday present ever. But we weren't going to get to go anywhere special for my ninth birthday, which would be his 35th.

For the last few years, Uncle Mark would put me on the back of his bike—an antique bike, a real Pre-cataclysm electric motorcycle—and we'd ride all the way into the city part of New Chicago that has been Chicago, even when Lake Michigan got high enough to flood the tall buildings. He'd take me for what they call Chicago Pizza at one of the places that had made it since forever. They would make a pizza, canine safe without onions, for us. A thick pizza that would fill me up with half a slice. Then we would ride up the lake shore for hours until it was time to come home.

Mommy would be mad because I'd be too full for the birthday supper she prepared. She was mad the first year. After that, she knew I'd be full, so she only made me a birthday cake.

This year, we wouldn't be doing that. Uncle Mark was at the rehabilitation center because he… as he would say when Mommy and Daddy weren't around, and we were outside in the snow once, so nobody there could hear: "Danny, I fucked up bad." I knew that was a bad word. But I also knew that was Uncle Mark telling me how bad a mistake he made by agreeing to bring bad stuff onto our ship. That was why he had to be in rehabilitation for two years, and why he could never go into space with us again.

Daddy had told me he'd take me for pizza on my birthday. But that almost didn't happen.

In early February, Daddy got off a call with his daddy, Grandpa. He walked into the kitchen where I was finishing my breakfast with Mommy. Krissy and Benji were in there working on homework on their tablets. I'd finished my most recent homework two days before, and was waiting for more to come from our school in Australia.

"I was talking to my dad and his caregivers," Daddy said. "They want us to come down to Phoenix."

He had tears in his eyes. I'd only seen Daddy cry a few times, and those were with Uncle Mark recently.

Mommy looked at him. "I'll get us tickets for tomorrow."

When we packed that night, Mommy made me pack my nice suit. I didn't know why I'd need that to go see Grandpa, but I packed it.

I didn't like visiting Grandpa. Grandpa was OK. But he smoked. And his cigarettes stank. It made everything in his little house—it wasn't even a house, but a part of a house—stink. And his fur stank. All his clothes stank. Parts of our ship still stank from Grandpa.

The next morning, we went to O'Hare Spaceport, but not to go to space. We didn't even take a suborbital. We had to take an airplane. They were like the worst parts of a suborbital and a shuttle. Like a suborbital, it never went straight up and only had lap belts. But it stayed really low in the atmosphere, 10,000 meters according to the pilot. That made the flight really, really bumpy. It was almost worse than being in zero-g.

We didn't stay at the hotel we usually stayed at near where Grandpa's tiny half-house was, but at a different hotel in a different part of the huge city of Phoenix. Phoenix was almost as big as New Chicago. It didn't have as many creatures, but it was even more spread out. And even in February, when New Chicago was all covered in snow, Phoenix was hot. So hot that if I were outside for more than a few minutes, I'd be panting hard. Some creatures sweat, but foxes can't. We have to pant.

"Dad, why aren't we staying in our normal hotel?" Benji asked as we drove into the new hotel's parking lot.

"This is closer to Grandpa's hospice."

"What is hospice?" I asked.

"It is where Grandpa is staying now."

————

Jason walked into the hospice alone. His family was still in the car parked under the shade structure. He hadn't fully understood why his father had moved from New Chicago out to the desert after he'd quit going to space. Winters in New Chicago weren't really any colder than space, and the housing service paid to keep roads and walks cleared, even for individuals and families who had opted for partial home ownership, like all of the Bartletts.

But Arthur Bartlett was stubborn, a trait he'd probably passed on to both of his sons. He insisted that he wanted to live out his last few decades somewhere warm with the same stubborn pride that he insisted that cigarettes were good for him, and reducing the symptoms of Spacers—the result of a life spent in variable gravity and exposed to the radiation that came from flying in poorly shielded freighters. Jason knew that cigarettes were no safer now than they had been centuries earlier, when they were killing humans by the millions, and humans were more than twice the size of a fox. Now, Arthur Bartlett was dying in his late 50s of lung cancer.

Before he talked to his father, he needed to speak to the caregivers.

Phoenix had been a place where creatures went to die, dating back long before the Cataclysm, so its hospice facilities blended medical necessity and patient comfort. But it still looked and smelled like a hospital full of dying creatures to Jason when he walked in the doors.

The receptionist, a porcupine in a simple dress, directed Jason to an office off to the side.

After a few minutes of waiting, the nurse in charge of his father's care came in. At first, Jason thought he was a pig or hog, then he realized he was a javalina.

"Mr. Bartlett, I am José Jaurez. I am in charge of your father's care."

"I have talked to your assistant on 2D a few times."

"Yes, I was on vacation for the last few weeks."

"How bad is my dad?"

"His last visit with the oncologist and his last scan were not good. The cancer has spread to most of his body. It's gotten into his brain. So far, it isn't impacting his cognitive abilities."

"How long?"

"This isn't an exact science, even with all of our technology. We've been treating cancer for centuries, and it still beats us far too often. Your father was a perfect case, a small canine spacer of his generation who smoked."

The javalina looked at Jason. "Have you upgraded the shielding on your ship?"

"It is beyond the current standards. I have three kits. I have shielding that exceeds what most of the fleet's ships have."

"Good, and you haven't been convinced that smoking will hold off Spacers?"

"Heavens no. I am still mad at that mongoose."

"I like to know that you won't be a future patient. Your father has a couple of weeks, maybe days. You should spend as much time as you can with him. You need to be prepared. Even if you've seen him on 2D, he looks bad. The supplemental oxygen isn't the worst of it. He's lost weight and fur, both from the chemo and from the cancer. He's nearly furless. I think he's been using a filter on his 2D calls."

"He has," Jason confirmed.

"At least we got him to quit smoking. We forced him to because it isn't allowed in the facility, and the nurses won't take him outside to smoke, not with supplemental O2."

"Regina and the kits will be happy. Especially Danny. He really hates the smell of smoke."

"Is your family with you?"

"They are out in the car, AC running. I can send a message to Regina and have them meet me in the lobby."

"I'll show you back to your father. You might want to warn the kits that their grandpa won't look like their grandpa."

———

Grandpa was all wrong. Grandpa was a red fox. Red foxes have red fur, or sometimes black fur, on their heads, backs, arms, legs, and even their ears and muzzle. And our tails, our brush as they are sometimes called, are supposed to be big and fluffy. Even at almost nine, my tail was big and fluffy. Mommy said I was going to have a spectacular brush since mine was already so fluffy.

But Grandpa had almost no fur. Just a tiny bit of red on the top of his head, and a few strands on his tail. He didn't look like grandpa. And he had something in his nose, and a tube under his shirt connected to a plastic bag hanging above his bed.

He didn't smell of stinky cigarettes anymore. He smelled worse. It smelled bad, but I couldn't say what it was. Not like poop or sick, but bad. Kind of like when food went bad, but different. Krissy and Benji could smell it too; I could see it on their faces. I don't know if Mommy and Daddy were hiding that they smelled it, or if they couldn't smell it at all. Sometimes grown-ups can't smell things that kits can.

"Jace, Reggie, I'm so glad to see you and the…" Grandpa started coughing even harder than he had the last time I'd seen him the year before. Once he recovered, he looked at us. "Benji, come and give your grandpa a hug."

Benji walked over to the bed and gave Grandpa a half-hug. My big brother seemed worried he might hurt him. Grandpa looked like he might break if squeezed too hard.

"So, Benjamin, are you stepping up to help out? You're thirteen, old enough to start applying for space operation licenses. I got my navigator's licence at thirteen."

Benji's tail dropped. Benji failed his navigation math class last year and had to retake it. He had trouble understanding how ships moved in space.

That math was easy for me. I could do his nav math homework, and he'd made me do it once. But Mommy found out. I was too young to get a license, so I couldn't help. Besides, I like sensors more than navigation.

Grandpa then looked at Krissy, who was in one of her flowery dresses. "And Krissy girl, are you doing what you can to help your mommy?"

"Mommy doesn't let us down in engineering. She says it's too dangerous for kits."

"Nonsense, I was crawling around those engineering spaces when I was your age, maybe even Danny's age."

"Arthur, the radiation given off by the reactors," Mommy said, glaring at Grandpa. The ship is shielded, but the reactors... even with their shielding. I make everyone in engineering carry tracking badges —including Ramon, or he's supposed to. That ferret never listens to me about his safety."

"A little radiation never hurt anyone."

Daddy looked at Grandpa, his ears flat. "Dad, radiation is a major cause of Spacers. Because I've put good shielding on the ship, better than was available when I was a kit, or when you were, Benji, Krissy, and Danny aren't going to get nearly as many symptoms of Spacers as you got."

"Jace, Spacers is just part of life. I lived with it for a decade and still worked. Quince gave me the trick to keep the symptoms at bay and kept me in space until I was almost fifty, nearly half a decade after most small spacers of my generation."

"And now you are dying two or three decades before most spacers of your generation because of the false cure that..." Daddy looked like he was trying hard not to say something. I bet it was the same word that Uncle Mark said when he and I were alone in the snow outside his rehab in Elgin/Dundee a few weeks earlier. "…mongoose."

Grandpa's ears went as flat as Daddy's, but then he started coughing very hard, even harder than he had before. A nurse, a coyote, came in and chased us out.

———

Regina looked at her tablet. She was supposed to be reviewing the kits' school work, but her mind kept drifting back to their abbreviated visit with Arthur Bartlett. She'd always gotten along with her father-in-law better than her own father. She'd gotten along with him better than his sons in some ways.

She'd met Jace and Mark when he'd first retired from space. But then, after Jace had spent six months in that Martian prison, he'd decided he had to come out of retirement and take back over. That was when he started that filthy habit. Quincy Monroe, a mongoose who lived in the other half of the duplex in Sun City, an ancient retirement community here in Phoenix that had been hosting old folks since the 20th century of the common human era, had told Art that smoking cigarettes could hold the most devastating symptoms of Spacers at bay.

For five years, even after Benji was born and she had asked, begged, and insisted that the smoke wasn't good for the baby, he continued to smoke on the ship. But finally, he had retired for good, trusting his sons with the operation of the family's legacy.

Now, he was dying. Jace had shared with her the news he'd gotten from the nurse that he could be dead within weeks or days. And instead of being able to say goodbye, every disagreement he had with his older son and with his daughter-in-law seemed to be getting in the way.

Benji walked up. "Mom, I need help with my navigation math. Grandpa is right. I need to figure it out."

Regina laughed. "Honey, I can balance reactor equations in my head, but trying to triangulate the vectors of launch between two bodies in the system might as well be another language."

She looked at him. "What is the problem?"

"A ship is at zero-g moving at 15,000 km/s and needs to target Earth, which is at parahelion, approaching your position 2,500,000 km away. Calculate the minimum and maximum thrusts to reach Earth with a three-week burn."

"Have you checked the orbit charts. They put Earth at perihelion because that makes its orbit easy. You only need to calculate how far it will move over three weeks and adjust accordingly. Then plug it into the navigator's equation."

"Mom, am I supposed to memorize the navigator's equation? We have a navigation computer on the ship. It has all the orbits of the major bodies logged. It uses the sensors to track the key stars. This isn't the last century when everyone was flying using their tails."

"Benji, you have to know how to do this. Computers can break down, even with backups. You have to master this, and that means memorizing the navigator's equation, knowing how to read the orbital tables for the major bodies, and at least understanding how the minor body tables differ from the major body tables, and how to use a basic calculator."

"Mom, I know how to use a calculator. I passed first-year maths when I was like five."

Regina rubbed the bridge of her nose. She could feel a headache coming on, which had nothing to do with raising a teenager and another one looming in less than three years.

"Can you try to work the problem now?"

"OK."

"And don't bug your little brother about it. He's working on his social studies right now."

"What if I offer to help him with his social studies. I could read his assignment to him."

She sighed. "Danny needs to practice his reading. The teachers say that we can't do too much of his reading for him."

With everything that happened, she hadn't been able to schedule the trip to Australia to take Danny for the special assessment that would let them confirm the reason he read slowly was an actual learning disability. She kept making excuses, she admitted that. Mark needed them close, then he needed their support at the trial. Then it was that bad storm at New Year's. Then Mark and Danny were spending a lot of time together, which the therapist and rehab said was important for Mark, and even if they took the suborbital, they would have to be in Australia for at least a week. And now Arthur was dying.

She knew Danny was smart, probably the smartest member of the family. And he was good at everything that didn't depend almost entirely on reading. That meant his social studies and English grades were bad, while his math, science, and engineering grades were so good that he was ahead of where most children of any species would be at almost 9.

"Mommy, can you help me with this bit?" Danny was tugging on her tail. That meant that she had lost track so hard that he hadn't been able to get her attention any other way.

"What is it, Kitto?"

He handed her his tablet. It was a passage talking about the convention after the Sentience Wars that established the UC.

"Mommy, the words keep changing, and I can't figure out what they are saying. Can you read it to me? Please. I've tried many times, and I keep getting more and more confused. Now my eyes hurt and my head hurts."

"Did you try reading it aloud, sounding out every word?"

"There are a lot of names, and a bunch of them have those funny characters because they were names that creatures gave themselves before we all decided to use human names."

"OK, but that means you'll have to read two chapters of your book today. I can't read it, and you can't get your brother, sister, or daddy to read it. And no cheating and sending it to Uncle Mark and having him read it to you either. He only gets so long on calls today, and he needs to spend time on his call with Grandpa."

"Is Grandpa dying. Is that why he smells bad? Is there something inside him that is killing him? Are we here to say goodbye to Grandpa?"

"Yes, honey, that is why we came down here. We don't know how long it will be before Grandpa dies."

"Is that why you, Daddy, and Grandpa got all angry this morning.

Because you won't have time to fight about everything, you have to finish all the fights you haven't had yet. Then you can be done with them?"

Regina looked at Danny—the wisdom of the kit. "Yes, Danny, I think you might be right. Daddy and I will go back to see Grandpa this evening, while Benji takes you and Krissy to the diner next to our hotel, does that sound OK?"

"You are going to let Benji watch Krissy and me? Are you sure he won't be mean and tie us up or something?"

"Benji will behave himself, or he'll lose his tablet for everything but homework until we get to space. And this is a secret between you and me: Benji has a boyfriend he texts all the time. He doesn't think Daddy and I know. He won't do anything that stops him from being able to text him until he's cut off."

She watched as Danny's ears went flat, and then he got that look that foxes get when they know a secret.

CHAPTER 2

"This is embarrassing." Benji glared at the booster seat as he climbed into it.

I climbed onto the booth seat across from him, then into my own hard plastic booster seat. Krissy climbed into her seat next to me.

The server, a coyote, set menus down in front of us, kits' menus for Krissy and me, and the grown-up menu for Benji.

"I want a Coke," Benji said before the server could walk away.

"Mommy doesn't let you have Coke," Krissy said.

"I'm in charge tonight, I can have a Coke."

"I'll have a water, but I want a straw," I let the server know. I was trying to be a good kit. I didn't want to get Benji in trouble, so he'd lose his tablet and not be able to talk to his boyfriend. I'd seen what happened to folks when they couldn't talk to their girlfriends and boyfriends in a lot of the old videos I liked to watch, and I didn't want Benji to have that happen. Benji was my big brother, which meant he could be mean, but it also meant he could be nice. Big brothers are... big brothers.

"I'll bring your drinks and be back to take your order."

I turned to look at the menu. This place was old, really old, pre-cataclysm. The booths were all made for humans, which is why even Benji needed a booster chair. Mommy and Daddy might need a booster. But the menu was good. They had hamburgers, pancakes, eggs with bacon, and they had hoppers. I hadn't had hoppers since we were on Mars. Mark had liked hoppers, too.

The server came back with our drinks. Benji's Coke was in a big glass. My water and Krissy's synthesized milk were in plastic glasses with lids.

"Any questions before I take your orders?"

I looked at him. "Are the hoppers good?"

"Nah, they are imported from the Midwest and have been kept near freezing for months. Half of them are dead already, and the rest have almost no hop in them. Best wait until summer or fall when they are fresh."

Benji looked at him. "I'll have the double burger, no toppings."

"I'll have the kit's burger and fries."

Krissy looked at him. "I'll have the chicken nuggets."

Throughout dinner, I watched as Benji kept looking at his tablet and then typed something. Every once in a while, he would wag his tail a lot. He had a goofy look on his face most of the time.

After she finished her chicken, but while I was still finishing up my burger, Krissy leaned over and whispered in my ear. "I think Benji has a girlfriend."

I leaned over and whispered back. "Mommy says it's a boyfriend."

"It's none of your business."

It was dark when we walked back to our hotel. The air smelled funny, like Phoenix always did.

When we got into our room, I lay on the bed and worked to read my book. At least the book didn't have all the confusing words and names that the social studies homework had. It was an old adventure story about someone named Robin Hood. I'd seen an old video where Robin Hood was a fox like me, but Mommy said that was made before the Cataclysm, when humans would make stories featuring animals like us, even before we were sentient. The Robin Hood in my book was a human. But I pictured him as a fox like the video. I pictured Maid Marian as a fox, too.

I didn't like the kissing scenes. I didn't understand kissing. I knew that having a boyfriend made Benji happy. Mommy made Daddy happy, and Daddy made Mommy happy. But Uncle Mark's girlfriends never made him happy. He seemed to be happier alone.

And, there were scenes in my videos that made me feel icky. When the humans—most of the videos I liked were Pre-Cataclysm because I liked those videos, I'm weird that way—would get really kissy and then start taking off their clothes. I knew they were doing something, something Mommy and Daddy said that they would explain when I got older, but it made me feel icky to think about getting that close with another creature that way.

I read about Robbin Hood until my eyes grew too heavy. I actually read three chapters. I'd have to answer all the questions tomorrow. But I liked to answer the questions the next day. One of the questions was always "How long ago did you read the chapter?" and if you answered "yesterday," you got more points for getting the answers right.

I turned off my tablet and curled into a tiny ball with my tail wrapped over my eyes. It wasn't like sleeping in my den on the ship, or at the house in New Chicago, but at least if I pushed myself against the pillow and pulled the blanket over me, it was cozy enough—or would be until Benji kicked me in the middle of the night, which he always did.

———

Jason looked at his dad. "Dad, we need to clear the air."

"I'm going to guess you are talking about the three of us deciding to fight in front of the kits this morning, not the stench I'm sure I'm making."

Jason had noticed a bit of an unpleasant odor in his dad's room, but nothing he'd call a stench.

Arthur continued. "Don't look at me with that blank expression— oh, you're losing your sense of smell already. Jace, that's one of the first things to go. First, the sense of smell, which is so key to us foxes, then you'll feel the tremors in your ears and tail. Son, I'm sorry I couldn't shield the ship when you were a kit. Your mom died when you were tiny, when Mark was even tinier. I had even less choice than you did about bringing my kits into space with me."

Jason sat in the chair at the head of his father's bed. "Dad, I wouldn't have given up one day in space with you. I know my sense of smell isn't what it once was. I know I'm showing the first signs of Spacers. I take a prescription, one given to me by the actual MD that I see every year for a physical, before we ship out for our annual run. She says it should keep the symptoms at bay enough to keep me flying for another decade or so."

Arthur laughed. "So about the same amount of time as your old fox. But at least they won't kill you a decade later. And they won't make your grandkits think you stink—at least if you don't start growing killer tumors inside your body."

Reggie looked at Jason's dad. "So, that slight smell is you?"

"Regina, my dear, I hope you are taking the same pills as your husband. One of my oncologists is a bloodhound. She still runs scans with her imaging thingamajiggy. But she also uses her nose. But I've seen the look on her face. I smell sick, I smell like I'm dying. All three of my grandkits could smell it when they came in here this morning. Benji tried to hide it. Danny never could keep his emotions off his face. Krissy, God love her, fought it, but in the end, she was as transparent as her little brother."

Jason looked at his father. "Dad, I'm sorry I was so hard on you about the cigarettes."

"Jason Bartholomew Bartlett. You have been right about those poison sticks for more than a decade. If your stubborn old father had gone to the doctors instead of listening to the weasel lookalike next door, I probably would be out there chasing tiny balls around a water-wasting lawn or some other activity that retired spacers do in this baking stretch of desert."

He then used the controls on his bed to sit up a bit more to look at Reggie. "Reggie, I'm sorry I argued with you about safety. You have always been the sensible one. Or at least most of the time. When I came out of retirement, I could tell you'd managed to mostly get my boys to think straight, even after Jace went and fucked up his first solo cargo run and got himself and his brother arrested.

Jason's ears went back. His dad couldn't ever let that rest for more than a few minutes, at least if the kits weren't around. And it was always his fault, because Mark was always his golden child, the kit who had survived when his wife died.

He'd never told his dad—he'd never told anyone, even Reggie— about those nights in the Martian prison. It was six Martian months, which are longer than six Earth months, each month lasting 55 or 56 sols. But it wasn't the almost an Earth year; it was his cellmate, Jesus Harper.

Jesus was a Maine Coon cat. He was as large, or larger than Jason. Just after lights out that first night, he hopped into Jason's cell and put his sharp teeth into the nape of Jason's neck and tore Jason's prison uniform off with his paws. And then he did something else... something Jason still didn't clearly remember, except he knew exactly what he forgot. That happened at least once a month. And it wasn't the worst thing that happened during that month.

Jason had moved past. But he always remembered it was Mark who had convinced him to carry the drugs, not the other way around. But his dad never saw it that way.

"Jason, are you even listening?"

He looked at his father. "Sorry, what were you saying?"

"Have you tried to get your brother a pass to come and see me?"

"I asked, but they won't give him a pass until he's earned enough credits, and that won't happen until he's been there for at least a year. And if he gets a pass, that would reset his credit count to zero, which might keep him in rehab after his two years. Mark wants to get out, even if he's grounded."

Art shifted to look Jason in the eye. "Why didn't you check that cargo contract yourself. You should have spotted that it was suspicious. My son is sitting in rehab and can't see his father in his last days because his captain couldn't keep him from loading explosives onto my ship."

Jason shot to his feet. "Dad, Mark was always the reckless one. Maybe it was because you spoiled him all the time. I know he grew up without a mother because she died when he was only a few days old. But I lost my mother when I was barely two. That is basically the same. I don't remember her any better than Mark does. I know that I have kept a much closer eye on what cargo I'm carrying than you did. I have never let anything actually illegal get on the ship since the drugs, and not just because I have a record."

He paced to the end of the bed and then back. "I happen to know that when I was fifteen and sixteen, we regularly ran counterfeit parts out to the belt. There were more than a few mining accidents up there around that time, thanks to the use of counterfeit parts. My social studies schooling, something you didn't pay that much attention to, included current events. I read about those. I told myself once the ship was mine, I might operate on the fringes, but I'd never put anyone in danger."

He walked back over and leaned down to look his father in the eyes. "Do you know what the drugs we—both Mark and I—were convicted of bringing to Mars were? It was a medicine that could not be synthesized on Mars at that time due to patent restrictions. One used to treat a common illness affecting construction workers building new domes. Martian law treats importation of that the same as any controlled drug. And the same cartels on Earth handle the pipelines because of it."

Jason's father looked at him. "Jason, I'm sorry. For years, I thought I put too much weight on you when I retired. I blamed myself for you ending up in a Martian jail for a year. I do love you as much as your brother. Don't think I don't."

Jason leaned over and carefully pulled his father into a hug. As he did, he could not help but notice the putrid odor of his father's cancer coming from all over his body.

I heard the door to our room open. It was dark, but I could see Mommy and Daddy coming in. Foxes can see in the dark, or at least in very low light. Benji hadn't closed the curtain all the way; it wasn't totally dark in our room. Mommy and Daddy seemed less angry at Grandpa, but they both looked sad.

Daddy walked into the head, the toilet, as it gets called, Earthside.

Mommy walked over to the couch where Krissy slept. Like me, she was curled into a tiny ball with her tail over her muzzle.

I'd told Krissy I could sleep on the couch since there were only two beds, but she said she didn't want to share a bed with a boy. So I had to share a bed with Benji, and she had to sleep on the couch.

Mommy pulled the blanket over Krissy a bit more.

Then she walked over to Benji, who was lying on his back, taking up as much of the bed as he could. He'd kicked off most of the blanket —even though he'd say I stole it, which was wrong, it was all down at the foot of the bed, and I only had a tiny corner over me where I lay up by my pillow. His white belly shone in the faint light. His tail was wrapped up over it, making it not quite as white. Mommy reached down and gave his chin a quick lick, which caused him to roll over onto his side and curl into a ball, but not as tightly as Krissy or me.

She then walked around to me. She bent down and whispered. "How are you doing, Danny?"

I let my tail slip off my muzzle.

"I saw you watching. Are you having trouble sleeping?"

"No, I woke up when you came in."

"Grandpa is doing OK. We're going back in the morning. They are going to see if we can visit him in the garden."

"He's still dying, isn't he?"

"Yes, honey."

"Can I be sad now, instead of when he's gone?"

"You can be sad now, and when he's gone."

"I'm going to cry now, OK."

"Don't wake your brother. He gets grumpy if he's woken up at night."

I rolled over, started stroking my tail, and crying as quietly as I could until I fell asleep.

The next morning, we went back to the hospice where Grandpa was. When we got there, he was sitting in a wheelchair in a garden. He was in the sun, but had blankets wrapped all around him. He still had the bag of clear liquid and the tank of air, and he still smelled.

"Danny, Krissy, Benji, how are you this morning?"

"I'm fine, Grandpa," I replied. My eyes still stung from crying the night before, and parts of my tail were still sticky from my nose. We didn't have time for me to take a bath because Benji had taken a shower that went on too long.

"I'm doing good, Grandpa," Benji replied. He sat on the edge of a planter next to where Grandpa was and pulled out his tablet. "Grandpa, can you help me with this problem. I'm having a bit of trouble with my navigation math."

Grandpa reached one of his bare paws over and scratched Benji between the ears. "Not good at navigation math, huh? Let's see if I can explain the old tricks for remembering the navigator's formula. There is an old poem, but I'm going to whisper it because your mom doesn't like it."

Grandpa then leaned over and whispered something in Benji's ear. Benji got a funny look on his face, then looked at his tablet and used his claw to write some numbers. "So the answer for this one would be… hang on… 0.5g to 0.7g?"

"See, it isn't that hard if you remember the formula. Of course, once the planet isn't at one of the easy points, and you are calculating the entire course, not just thrust, it gets a bit harder. But the navigator's formula is the important bit."

"But Grandpa, that way of remembering it is… rude. And I like boys, not girls."

"Oh, my oldest grandson is into boys, is he? Well, can I tell you a secret? Did you know I had a boyfriend before I met your grandma? And I had a couple after she died. I like both boys and girls. There is a tod here who works as an orderly who, if I wasn't dying and he wasn't barely older than my grandkits…"

"Grandpa, that is… is it that handsome fella over there pushing the antelope back inside? Oh, he'd be quite the catch."

I turned to see a silver fox, which is just a red fox with black or silver fur, pushing an antelope in a wheelchair back into the building from the garden. I couldn't see what either Grandpa or Benji saw in him. He was handsome, I guess.

"Krissy, so you need help with homework or something from your old Grandpa?

Krissy walked over and stood by him. "Grandpa, you aren't old. You are 59, that isn't old."

"Kristine Amelia Bartlett, I can't get out of bed and into a wheelchair without help. I need someone to take me to the bathroom. That makes me old, even if the calendar doesn't."

"Grandpa, I don't want you to die." She started crying and then leaned into his chair. He began rubbing her back and stroking her head.

I sat there watching until she quit, wiped her muzzle on her arm, and looked at him. "Grandpa, I love you. I'll miss you."

"I'm not dying today, Krissy, I promise."

She walked over and wrapped her arms around Daddy.

I walked over. Grandpa's stink was even worse this close. I tried not to wrinkle my nose. I didn't want Grandpa to think I was even more bothered by this than I was by his cigarettes. But his cancer smelled worse somehow.

"Hi, Grandpa."

"Danny, I'm sorry I smell bad. I know you don't like bad smells. I can't help it. The sickness inside me and the medicine that is trying to keep it from growing too fast all make me smell bad. I can't smell it, 'cus smell is the first thing that goes from Spacers when you're a fox. But your Mommy and Daddy have made the ship a lot safer for you than it was when I flew on it. You might not ever get Spacers."

"Really? I thought everyone got Spacers."

He laughed, which turned into bad coughing, bad enough that his nurse, a big jack hare, came up and helped.

"Danny, nobody wants to get Spacers. We all tried to shield the ships. We all tried to find ways to avoid the other things that contribute. The fleet makes its creatures use something they call a spin and puke if they have to be on the Moon or Mars for too long."

Spin and puke, that didn't sound good.

"What is a spin and puke?"

"It is like a tiny habitat ring. It's kind of like how you have to spend half your year here on Earth, so your bones and muscles develop correctly."

"Daddy wants to put artificial gravity on the ship as soon as he can. Then maybe we could stay in space year-round."

"I'd love to see that. But artificial gravity is still experimental."

I reached into my satchel, pulled out my tablet, and opened the article. I had read it often enough, wanting to make sure I really had read it right, so I had it where I could find it. "This article in *Science for Kits* says that they ran successful experiments on Ceres, and that it should be ready for production soon."

He used his paw to guide my tablet to where he could read it. "Wow, real artificial gravity like on all the old human SciFi videos I used to watch with you when you came for visits."

My tail started wagging. I didn't like how Grandpa stank from cigarettes, but he was the only grown-up, other than Uncle Mark, who had ever sat with me to watch *Star Trek* or any of those other old human videos.

"Grandpa, can we watch one now?"

"Maybe a short one. Not a long one, OK? I'm going to need to go inside soon. I need help to…" He leaned into my ear. "…use the head."

I found one of my favorite short episodes, only twenty minutes long. It was one of the ones that was drawn—animated—but it was good.

After that, Grandpa had to go inside, so we went back to our hotel room.

———

Mark looked at his father through the screen. The last time he'd seen his father on the screen, a few days before, he'd looked more normal. But then Jace had sent him the note that Dad had been using filters on his calls.

"Dad, I'd be there if I could. But they won't let me out, even for a dying parent. You should know that. The rules of rehabilitation are strict; I'm only allowed out for very specific reasons."

"You could go halfway around the world to tell everyone that a human had duped you into putting your whole family in danger, but you can't fly halfway across the continent to see your old fox one last time before he dies."

Mark's ears went flat. "Dad, I had to testify against her. That was part of my plea agreement. They were going to levy terrorism charges against me."

"That is what they told you to get you to agree to cooperate. The most they could have convicted you of was endangering, and a good lawyer, maybe not that fleet jackal but one who actually was interested in protecting an honest spacer, might have even gotten you off."

Mark took a deep breath in through his nose and let it out through his mouth, then repeated the process. Calls were monitored. Losing his temper at his dying father would not help. He could even get demerits or lose points.

"Dad, can we not fight. I feel bad enough about everything already. I'm sorry, I am not the golden child you always thought I was. I was always the fuck up." Damn it. That might be a demerit right there. "You just never saw it. I've always been the one pushing boundaries. If I didn't push Jace into carrying grey market cargo, he'd have stayed entirely in the white even if it had driven him out of business. I was the one who made the drug deal that got him sent to prison for six Martian months. Nearly every bad thing that happened to this family since Mom died has been my fault."

He closed his eyes. "Even Mom's dying was probably my fault. She got sick delivering me after all. Maybe you should have blamed me for that, instead of treating me like something precious that you had left over after losing her."

His father looked at the screen and started to say something, but it was lost in a coughing fit so hard that he accidentally cut the connection. By the time Mark managed to get a connection back to the hospice in Phoenix, the nurse told him, "I'm sorry, Mr. Bartlett, but Mr. Bartlett isn't available right now."

His heart sank. Had his dad died. Were his last words to him—the last words his father ever heard going to be his angry words about the mother he never knew, the mother he could never have known?

He looked at the clock in his room. It was still early. He could still go to the gym. He left and walked to the gym as fast as he could without running, which was forbidden in the halls. The gym was quiet, even though it was evening free time. He was able to find a cycle. He climbed on and started peddling. He peddled and just kept peddling, turning up the tension so that it was just hard enough. He worked until he wasn't just tired, but too tired to think, to care, to even feel.

Then he went back to his room, lay down on his bed, and curled into a ball like he did when he was a kit. He even laid his tail over his muzzle and his eyes. He cried for the first time in far too long. He cried about his dad dying or being dead. He cried about losing access to space. He cried about his lost arm. He cried about missing his family. He cried, saying he hated himself for making so many mistakes. He cried because he needed to cry. He cried himself to sleep for the first time in over twenty years.

CHAPTER 3

The next several times we went to see Grandpa, he was just lying in his bed. He looked like he was sleeping. But he had a big tube in his mouth connected to a machine that hissed a lot. Daddy and Mommy cried a lot. We all cried a lot.

Mommy and Daddy had meetings with the doctors and Uncle Mark, who had to call in from the rehabilitation center in Elgin/Dundee. When those happened, we'd have to stay back at the hotel. Benji would try to act like he was doing fun things with us, like taking us to the hotel's pool.

One day, three days after the last time we saw Grandpa awake in the garden, he took us to a big water park while Mommy and Daddy went to see Grandpa and meet with the doctors.

That would have been fun, except we were all really sad.

When we got back to the hotel, with our fur all wet, matted, and smelling of pool water, Mommy and Daddy were really sad.

"I'm sorry, kits," Daddy explained. "Grandpa died today. We were talking about how to proceed, and his heart stopped."

My eyes started burning right then. I curled up on the floor into a ball and cried until bedtime, I think. I didn't have dinner that night.

A few days later, I had to put on my suit, the one Mommy had made me pack. We all got into a big black car, all sitting in the back. Daddy had a jar in his lap, like how I carry Mommy's sourdough jar when we go between Earthside and space. But I knew that jar held what was left of Grandpa.

The car drove us to a large field with many small, flat, square stones. We walked out a long way until there was a hole. A few other creatures were gathered there. Most were dressed nicely. I recognized a few as Grandpa's neighbors from Sun City. There were also a few other spacers we'd worked with. And there was an old badger there in robes.

Daddy and Benji carefully put the jar with Grandpa into the small hole that had been dug. Then the badger in robes said a few things about Grandpa. Then the spacers all started singing an old song about how spacers always return to space, even when they are in the ground.

We then went back to the car and to a big hall, where many of the same creatures were sitting around and talking about Grandpa. Some of them talked to me. But a lot of them just ignored me. They knew Grandpa, and I was just one of his grandkits.

———

Two days after his dad's funeral, Jason and the family headed back to New Chicago. It was already the middle of March, and he'd need to head down to the South American spaceport so he could take the stalk up and meet with the tug that was bringing their freighter from storage on Luna. There would be winter maintenance to inspect, guest crew to hire, and cargo to contract for or purchase before they could head up to Mars or to one of the locations in the belt.

When they arrived at the Phoenix airport—as big a city as Phoenix was, it didn't have a spaceport, and its airport only handled a few suborbitals—he looked at their flight reservations on his tablet and noticed the date, March 15. He looked over at Danny, who was starting to recover from his dad's death, even if he was the kit who started grieving first. Jason was only beginning to fully accept that his father was gone himself.

Tomorrow was Danny's ninth birthday. It was also Mark's 37th birthday, and it would be the first time in 8 years that the pair wouldn't celebrate it together. Jason had promised to do what he could, and then his dad went into hospice, and the last two months of their Earthside time were thrown off plan. When they got home, he needed to do all of the tasks that would be easier from his home than from a hotel. He couldn't be going to his brothers and trying not to kill himself and his youngest son on a motorcycle. He couldn't be trying to find the right pizza place downtown. He couldn't be taking a long ride up the lakeshore.

Just before their flight to O'Hare was called, he looked at the weather for New Chicago for the next day. Spring in Chicago could be unpredictable. Maybe there would be a blizzard—just his luck, sunny with a high near 20, perfect weather for taking a motorcycle ride with a nine-year-old fox kit.

He spent the flight doing as much as he could, composing the postings for the job boards about the guest positions on the ship.

"Reggie, are you sure that the Gibbs aren't coming back?"

His wife leaned over from where she was watching the three kits across the aisle. "Yes, they were both rather upset about us getting boarded and unknowingly carrying explosives. I had to pay them extra to avoid Lauryn filing a complaint with the Engineering Guild."

"But you are sure Ramon is sticking around."

"Honey, I think Ramon might have spent the winter on the ship, even with it in the storage and maintenance yard. I don't know when he last left our ship."

"Even after Mark shot him."

"Jace, I think Mark shooting him to keep him from murdering fellow fleeters made him respect us more. You have to think like a fleeter, even a traumatized and disgraced one."

"So, we're looking for a co-pilot/navigator who can also cover sensors when the automated systems aren't enough, and two engineering mates. And our pay rates are near the bottom, maybe even worse, since we'll probably not make enough to cover expenses. We might even have to take some UC belt runs, and those are costs only."

"You could exaggerate the costs enough to pay a bit more on the UC contracts."

"That is fraud. I'm in no hurry to become Mark's roommate."

Regina laughed. "I think the rehabilitation centers are single occupancy. At least they allow for congagal visits."

"We haven't… not since the miscarriage."

"I think I'm ready again. And you know how I get in space, and I know how you get in space."

"Are you protected, or are we going to run the risk…"

"The doctor says if we are even thinking of another kit, we should run with the safeties off."

"How long have you had your safeties off?"

"About a year now."

"So, you were thinking…"

"I figured either I was out of fuel, or another kit would be good. I know Danny is nine, but he's not too old to become a big brother."

"Benji will be the bigger problem. He'll be convinced you are doing it because he's a teenager—or because he's gay."

"If Benji doesn't know we accept him the way he is, he hasn't paid any attention. In fact, we should insist we meet this boy he's been texting constantly before we go spaceside."

"But not tomorrow. Tomorrow, I have to go to Mark's and see if I remember how not to kill myself on a motorcycle."

Regina looked at him. "You aren't going to try to take Danny out on your brother's death machine, are you?"

"Do you have a better idea?"

"Take the train downtown. It's a lot safer. Danny will understand. You are not your brother, don't try to be. The pizza and the effort will be good enough. Trust me."

He leaned over and gave his wife a quick lick. "OK, I'll trust you. But if he's in one of his sad moods when we get back, it's your fault."

———

I woke up early on my birthday. I was nine. But I wouldn't get to go downtown on the back of Uncle Mark's motorcycle. Even when I turned eight, and it was snowing, but not hard, he had me put on my warm coat and scarf. With that and the special helmet that Uncle Mark had just for me, I was warm the whole way downtown, and all the way along Lake Michigan, and then back home. Only my tail, which I let fly behind us like Uncle Mark did, and the tips of my ears, which stuck up through the holes in the helmet, got cold.

I crawled out of my little wooden den into my big bedroom. The sun was coming in through my bedroom window, which looked east. I climbed up on the desk and looked out. If I shaded my eyes to cover the sun, I could see the big buildings downtown. I could see the two tall buildings that had been built way before the Cataclysm. One time when we were downtown, Uncle Mark took me up in the taller one. It wasn't like being in space, but I could see all over the city. I could even see out to the part of the city where our house was, which they used to call the suburbs. I could see the old freeways, most of which were gone, except for small bits like where Uncle Mark had his house.

Uncle Mark's house was under a bit of an old freeway that still stood. Birds and bats lived on top of that bit, and land creatures like foxes lived in houses underneath. His house was small, with only a kitchen, a head, and his small bedroom, which was more like a fox's den than Mommy and Daddy's bedroom or even Benji's bedroom.

But on my ninth birthday, which was also Uncle Mark's 35th birthday, he was still in the Elgin/Dundee criminal rehabilitation facility. They didn't let creatures out of those places for their birthdays. The law said they had to stay in there at least as long as the judge said, and then, when the folks who ran the facility said they had completed their rehabilitation. Uncle Mark would be 37 when he was released. We'd miss two birthdays together.

I was still sad about Grandpa dying, too. I'd been sad about Grandpa for a few weeks, even before he died. Mommy said I could be sad about that for a long time. She even said I might be angry, or other things at times, and that was OK. Part of me was glad I wouldn't have to be around his stinky cigarettes, but then when I thought that, I got sad again.

I stopped looking out the window and climbed down off the desk. I got clean underwear, a clean t-shirt, and clean pants out of my drawers. I really wanted to put on a jumpsuit. Pants weren't practical. They didn't have big pockets to put things in. My pants had pockets.

Mommy only got me what they called cargo pants. But they never had enough pockets for all the things I wanted to carry. I had to carry a satchel to hold my tablet while planetside. But Mommy insisted that jumpsuits were only for when we were on the ship, or at least in space.

So I put on my pants.

My t-shirt was a *Doctor Who* shirt. They had just started taking the ancient videos and converting them to 3D. They took the old human 2D, but instead of just making it 3D like they did with some things, they kept the voices and replaced all the characters with others. The Doctor, who had always looked human, and all his human friends were now various other species.

My t-shirt featured the new Fourth Doctor, a linx with tufted ears and a colorful scarf that ran all around the shirt, even to the back. I thought the shirt was neat, in part because it took one of my favorite old human videos and made it something that folks who didn't like old human videos could appreciate.

Once I was dressed, I went downstairs to the kitchen. Mommy was making eggs and bacon. I could tell that she'd gotten real eggs instead of synthesizing them. She must have taken the trolley to the nearby market really early to get them, since we didn't get back from Phoenix until late in the afternoon the day before. But she knew I really liked real eggs.

"Good morning, Danny. And happy birthday."

"Thank you, Mommy."

"Are you feeling OK this morning?"

"I'm good."

"Your eggs are almost ready. I'm making them over hard, just like you like them."

My tail started wagging. Synthesized eggs were always scrambled, unless they were synthesized cooked, and Mommy didn't like synthesizing cooked food when she didn't have to.

"And I'm getting the bacon crisp. The bread is from the market, but it is real bread, or at least it is baked bread, not bread made by a synthesizer."

"I know you didn't have time to bake bread."

Daddy came downstairs. "Happy birthday, Kitto." He leaned over and gave the top of my head a quick lick.

"Thank you, Daddy."

Benji came downstairs, carrying his tablet so close to his muzzle I don't know how he didn't trip. His tail was wagging, and he had that goofy look on his face that told me he was already texting, or maybe even in a 2D call with his boyfriend.

He looked at me as he walked past. "Oh, happy birthday, Danny. Trent says 'Happy Birthday,' too."

"Thank you, Benji. So Trent is your boyfriend."

Benji nearly dropped his tablet. "I didn't… Yes, Trent is my best friend… But I am really fond of, OK. Mom, Dad, Danny, I am very fond of Trent, who lives down the street."

Krissy walked in. "So Benji does have a boyfriend."

She then ran her paw backwards through the fur on the top of my head. "Happy birthday, Danny."

———

Mark walked into the PT gym. Four months at the Elgin/Dundee Criminal Rehabilitation Center, nearly five months after having his arm shot off by the human sniper who wanted to kill him and Pat Bass to keep them from testifying against Xandra Mathias, two months after getting his first temporary prosthetic, and he still had an hour of physical therapy on his schedule every day. He guessed that a routine day would be a good distraction from the fact that it was his birthday, a day he'd normally spend with Danny. Danny was still his favorite birthday present.

He could still remember his 24th birthday. He'd been over at Jace and Reggie's house. They'd planned a quiet celebration for his birthday that evening after the two kits had gone to bed. Benji was five, Krissy was two, and Reggie was nine months pregnant, so anything wild was out of the question. Not that they had ever done anything wild for any of their birthdays. They were spacers, so celebrations, even when planetside, were muted. Maybe a dinner out and cake.

But then, about the time Jace was programming supper into the synthesizer, since Reggie wasn't in shape to cook, and neither of the tods had learned how, Reggie confessed that she'd been in labor for several hours and it had reached the point that, since they weren't in the middle of space thrusting like they were the first two times she'd delivered, she should probably go to the hospital and deliver safely for once.

That left him alone with the two younger kits until it was time to call for a car and bring them to meet their younger brother. He'd met Danny around 2200 on his 24th birthday and had been instantly smitten with the tiny bundle of fur—not that Danny had much fur when he was a newborn.

Now he was stuck in rehab, where the only acknowledgement of his birthday might be someone mentioning it when, if they called him in the evening during the time when calls were allowed. In every other way, today would be like every other day had been since he'd arrived in the middle of the previous November, like every day would be until he was released in another 19 months as long as he didn't mess up and not complete his rehabilitation program. And that rehabilitation program included the physical rehabilitation of the injury sustained between his arrest and his day in court.

He walked into the gym to find Oklee Morrow, his baboon PT, waiting for him.

"Good morning, Mark. How is your prosthetic doing today?"

"It is functioning fine. No unexpected discomfort when I put it on this morning."

"Why don't you hop onto the hand cycle and get warmed up. Then we'll work on your strength and flexibility. And I think you are due for a cybernetic control and sensitivity assessment, so we can check the programming again. Your updated temporary prosthetic is scheduled to be ready in three weeks, and we want to make sure it is programmed correctly."

Mark's ears dropped a bit. The control and sensitivity assessments were a long, slow process of checking every connection to ensure he had complete control over the cybernetic prosthetic's capabilities. There were hundreds, or even thousands, of individual connections just in the paw. The last assessment nearly resulted in a demerit because he was late for his laundry shift.

He settled into the hand bike, putting his real paw on one handle and his prosthetic paw on the other. He noted that he couldn't feel the right pedal as well as the left, something he'd need to report to the cybernetic tech when it came to the analysis. He started cranking and pushed up to a steady 20 rpm, the pace that Oklee liked him to maintain for the 15-minute warm-up period.

Once warmed up, he went to the bench, where he did a series of shoulder lifts and other exercises for another 10 minutes or so.

Then he went back to the cybernetics office at the back of the gym. The cyber tech, Madalynn Lynn, was a young fennec fox. She was tiny, but had an attitude that made up for being hardly bigger than a mouse.

"So, Mr. Bennet, how have you abused your arm this month?

"It's Mark Bartlett, and you can call me Mark. And I've been doing everything you tell me, taking it off at night, charging it daily. Cleaning it. Not using it as a club or a tool other than within its design parameters…"

"OK, that is what I like to hear. Let me plug into the diag port, and we'll see how it is doing."

"I think the pad sensitivity has dropped. I noticed when I was on the bike this morning…"

CHAPTER 4

Daddy and I left the house not long after breakfast. We walked to the end of the block and got on the trolley. In New Chicago, they called these trolleys; in other cities, the same vehicles were called trams or streetcars. Our trolley took us to the center of our part of the city, which Daddy said had once been its own town before the Cataclysm, but was still part of Old Chicago because of how the human government worked. It had some weird name like Palatine, but it was now just part of New Chicago.

We caught the train, but not the one that we took to O'Hare. This train continued all the way to downtown.

Downtown Chicago was a lot of really tall buildings, most built long before the Cataclysm. Many of them still showed how the lake had once risen high enough to flood them. My social studies class said that the Great Lakes didn't rise as much as the oceans before and during the Cataclysm, but they still rose—something about the flooding of the Saint Lawerance Seaway and increasing rains.

Once we got off the train, we walked. It was a nice spring day, so walking was pleasant.

Downtown New Chicago has lots of different kinds of creatures, all rushing everywhere. They don't always pay attention to two red foxes.

We're not the biggest creatures around. We're a lot bigger than mice, voles, and shrews, but we're smaller than wolves, tigers, deer, horses, and other big creatures. I nearly got squished by an elephant who was rushing down the sidewalk, paying more attention to the 2D call he was making on the tablet held in his trunk than where he was walking. Daddy had to pull me out of his way.

I had to help Daddy find the right pizza restaurant. But their sign outside says they make "Authentic Chicago Deep Dish" and "Proudly in Operation Since The Human Common Era." This was where Uncle Mark always took me.

The server, a rat with a fancy bow on his tail, led us back to a table with chairs sized for medium-sized creatures like foxes, with wide backs so our tails fit through without any trouble. He then recommended that we get appetizers since our pizza would be about forty minutes.

Daddy nodded, and we got a small plate of tiny fried meatballs made with real pork and beef while waiting for our pizza.

"Danny, I know you wanted to come down here with Mark."

"It's OK. He has to be in rehab. He… he told me he fucked up by making that deal."

Daddy laughed. "That sounds like Mark. Don't let your mom hear you use that word, OK."

"OK. Daddy, why did Uncle Mark make a bad deal?"

"He was worried. It costs a lot to run our ship, but we want to stay spacers."

"Some folks just stay on Earth or Mars. I don't think Benji's friend Trent's parents do anything."

I knew who Trent was. His family had lived on our street as long as I could remember. He and Benji had been friends for a long time, so Trent being Benji's boyfriend seemed right to me.

"A lot of folks are willing to live in houses that they got from their parents, and on synthesized food. It is a fine life. But if you want more in life, you need a job. There is only so much you can get on a basic income. And we're spacers, we want to go to space."

I thought about not being in space, even if zero-g makes my tummy feel funny, and I hate having to use the zero-g toilet.

"Daddy, is there a way to make the zero-g toilet hurt less?"

"Danny, it hurts a bit less as you get bigger, but it sucks a lot, and we have little..." Daddy looked around, then leaned in close so he could speak softly into my ear. "...penises. They are kind of sensitive. Everyone's can be. I'll try to get some softer, small attachments and some gel that might help, OK."

"I'm going to really try to use it this year, and not rely on having to wear a diaper. I don't like stinking all the time."

"That is good. I still don't like using the zero-g toilet either. Most males don't."

I laughed. "You told me."

"But don't put off using it, I'm not helping you clean up the head, and your mom isn't either. If you have an accident in there, you are doing all the cleaning. And I'm not going to thrust until it is cleaned."

"OK, Daddy. I promise."

When our pizza arrived, I ate almost an entire slice before I was too full to eat more. Daddy ate an entire slice. We got the other two slices boxed up to take home. We then walked out to the lakeshore and watched the water for a while.

"Danny, I love being in space, but Earth is the only place in the solar system that has open water like this. Seeing water, seeing folks out there on the water in their boats... Did you see the folks out there in the sailboats?"

"Yes."

"Before humans ever tried to fly in space, or even in the air, they crossed the oceans in sailboats using nothing but the wind. They had to use the stars they could see from here on Earth to navigate."

"We still use stars to navigate. That is how we know where we are. The planets all move, but the stars stay in the same place... or close enough that we can figure out our position by them, no matter what happens. Every time we go to zero-g, the ship or the navigator identifies the location of the sixty most important stars and uses that to figure out where we are in relation to Sol and the major bodies."

Daddy ruffled the fur on the top of my head. "Navigating by the stars across the oceans was similar. But they didn't have computers;

they had only simple brass instruments. You remember that thing I brought home from Grandpa's house?"

"I think so. He had it hanging on his wall."

"That was an old mariner's sextant. A real Pre-cataclysm antique. More than a thousand years old. I'm going to hang it in your bedroom when we get home. You are a natural navigator and sensor operator. In four years—four years from today, you are going to sit your exams."

"Daddy, I'll… I'll be thirteen four years from today."

"That is when you can sit for both the sensors' and navigator's exams. You'll be ready for both by then. I don't see why you shouldn't get your licenses then. You are a natural-born spacer. Your brother and sister are too, but you are the one who is going to prove it. Benji will probably realize he can get his co-pilot's licence soon enough and then beg me to take the exam, but I'm not going to push him. But he won't get his navigator's license until he passes nav maths two."

"He hasn't passed nav maths one yet."

Daddy looked at his watch. "We'd better head back to the station if we don't want to miss the train. Mommy is making you a cake, carrot —your favorite flavor. And your brother is waiting to steal the rest of this pizza."

———

Ramon stirred from his berth. Someone was buzzing at the main lock. At least this time, they remembered that he was on the ship and were giving him time to get dressed.

In December, one of the contractors who came aboard to install the upgraded coms that the UC was putting into all ships just walked in to find Ramon in his bunk sleeping the way he did whenever he thought he was alone—not that he had much to hide. Ferrets weren't what anyone would call well-endowed, and he had long fur for a ferret, so he could almost pass as a non-sentient ferret when naked. But it was the principle—you didn't walk into someone's home without warning.

He quickly pulled on his jumpsuit, one of the same two he'd been wearing for years, with the shadows of his old rank insignia—he might go back and put on underwear if he got a chance—and then dropped down the ladder to the rec deck and checked the screen. Two otters were standing there in the uniforms of the port workers' guild. He pressed the button to open the outer lock door and, after confirming that the pressures were the same, opened the inner lock door.

"Permission to come aboard," the lead otter asked, pausing at the threshold of the inner door.

"It's not my ship. I'm just the maintenance tech who stays on board even when it is put into storage."

"You know that Luna port has UC housing available."

"Why would I do that when I have a perfectly good berth here?"

"Whatever, Chief."

"It's FTC. We're here to take this boat to the barge that will take it to Preston Station."

"Thruster tanks are all topped off."

"I know, Chief, we have the port maintenance and upgrade records right here." The otter tapped her tablet.

Ramon reached his left paw over to tap his shoulder where the shadow of his insignia was. "Only this stripe was there when I was discharged. The rest were gone. I was an FTC, not a Chief. I lost the right to be called chief. I probably lost the right to be called FTC, so call me Ramon, OK."

"All right, Ramon. We're heading up to the bridge. It should only take us about 30 minutes to load this boat onto the barge. Once we're done, we'll hook the all-ship coms up to the barge systems so you'll get notifications, and we'll let the barge know you are here so they won't dump you in the dark."

"Thank you."

It had been a long winter. Most winters were quiet. But this year, Ramon had spent more time reading news feeds. He'd been upset about Mark shooting him, until he realized that the borders were fleeters. The idea that he might have killed a fleeter thinking that it was a pirate, or that he might have killed the Bartlett kits to save them from pirates when it was just fleeters coming to arrest Mark and remove the explosives he'd accidentally allowed on board… If he ever saw that fox again, he'd have to thank him. But Ramon was never going Earthside, and Mark couldn't come into space, or at least not onto the ship.

Ramon didn't plan on leaving the ship for more than essential needs until… he had his exit planned, but he didn't think that would happen for quite a few years.

He'd left the ship a few weeks ago to see a doctor on Luna. He'd given Ramon some medicine to help with his Spacer's symptoms, and they had helped a lot. He could smell more than he had in years. And the tremors were gone. He might even start carrying the radiation dose gauge that Regina Bartlett insisted he carry when down in engineering space, and make sure his exposure stays below the limits for any day, week, and month—maybe.

Since he was up anyway, he grabbed the dose gauge and headed down to engineering. The winter maintenance crews had spent a lot of time down there, and he needed to make sure that they hadn't broken anything important. They were supposed to be installing new shielding around the reactor and the output piping. But there was plenty down in those spaces they could have broken.

As he worked, he thought about all the other work that was done. The new coms gear was interesting. When the UC took control of MarsTech, they discovered that it had been sitting on technology that allowed reliable communications with ships at thrust. They had quickly moved to install that on as many ships as possible.

When he was done inspecting engineering, he headed up to the bridge where the two otters were flying the ship, performing the final docking maneuvers to load it into the barge. He nodded before vectoring himself to check the whole comms box. He could see the newly installed equipment. Equipment developed and used by the very terrorist who had tricked a member of his crew, his family, into carrying explosives as part of an elaborate plot to put the human minority in charge of the solar system, which would now be used to improve the lives and safety of not only the family he adopted, but of every spacer across the solar system.

The old ferret, the former fleet maintenance chief, before he'd been busted down to Fleeter Third Class and then given a less-than-honorable discharge, looked at the equipment and thought that was a fitting legacy for hate and terror.

———

Daddy left a few days after my birthday. He took the suborbital down to the base of the South American stalk and then took a pod up to Preston Station. He preferred to depart from Preston Station in the spring. If we departed from Luna, we'd have to take a shuttle from O'Hare to the moon, and that limited what we could take from our Earthside house. Some of the things we liked to take back and forth, like Mommy's sourdough mother, weren't allowed on the shuttles up to Luna. We could take them from Luna, but not to Luna due to the way that Earth Launches worked.

I'd only launched from Earth once. That was when I was six, and we had to go down to Earth for a few weeks in the middle of our time in space because Grandpa hurt himself playing golf. When we went back to space, we took a launch, which is kind of like a suborbital until it goes straight up, like launching from Mars.

The rest of us stayed on Earth for two more weeks to get everything ready for space. That meant a lot of packing and shopping. Both Benji and I needed new jumpsuits. We'd both outgrown our old jumpsuits.

One afternoon, Mommy took all of us to the mall, where we went to Spacer's Supply.

Since we took the trolley to get there, Trent followed us, holding hands with Benji the whole way. I even saw them kissing and licking when we were about halfway to the mall.

Krissy leaned over. "Now that everyone knows Trent and Benji are boyfriends, they are just showing off."

Spacers Supply claimed to have everything a spacer needed, but they mostly had clothing. They had really nice jumpsuits in all sizes and shapes. I picked out several in light blues and greens, and some in a red I thought looked nice.

Trent walked over and handed me a cream jumpsuit. "Buddy, you should try this one on. I think it would look good on you."

I looked at him. "You are Benji's boyfriend."

"That doesn't mean I think his little bro should look bad. You are cute too, in an annoying little brother way."

My tail gave a weird little wag. I didn't want to have him lick me or kiss me. That was gross. But having someone like how I looked felt good.

I had to try on my jumpsuits three times before I found the right size, and to make sure that they were long enough and loose enough. But in the end, I had six new suits: two light blue, one green, one red, and two in cream, as Trent suggested.

Mommy then took us to the food court. I had a burger with a shake. It was all synthesized right in front of me, but it was still OK.

Benji and Trent were still all licky and kissy to the point that Krissy kept telling them to "Knock it off," and "get a room," but Mommy didn't seem to mind.

We then went home.

———

Regina looked at their space bags. Everything, well almost everything, was packed, ready to be taken to O'Hare Spaceport in the morning. They'd need to hire a car to take them, since taking four large bags plus their carry-ons, including the old mason jar with her sourdough mother, which was packed carefully into Danny's bag, was more than she even wanted to think about trying to get onto the trolly from their neighborhood, to the station in the center of the region, and then onto the train to O'Hare. It would be much easier to just have the hire car with its large trunk bring them.

The kits were in their rooms. When she'd checked, Krissy and Danny were in their dens with the lights off.

Benji was lying on his bed, on his belly, with his tablet propped up, watching something. From the way he was moving and a slight odor, he seemed to be… He might have been on a call with Trent, and if so, Jace needed to have a strongly worded talk about what was appropriate to be doing during calls with his boyfriend. She also needed to double-check that Benji hadn't managed to bypass the house's firewalls to gain access to certain materials. Not that she objected in principle, but not for her thirteen-year-old son. Not yet. He could use his imagination, just like she had.

She went into her bedroom and picked up her tablet. Jace was already at Preston Station on board the ship. He sent her four résumés to consider as potential engineering mates.

She looked through them. She rejected two right away. One was clearly created by an AI as a cover for someone who wasn't qualified. If she checked, she was sure that the spaceship engineering licence tied to that name would either come back as revoked, stolen, or for someone dead or in rehab of one sort or another.

The other was for a known drug head. Jace should have recognized the name, but maybe he didn't keep up with the bad engineers.

But the other two looked good. Jackson "Jax" McDonald was a jack hare with a good record, but a bum paw from a recent burn. He'd do just fine as her first engineering mate. Peter Reynolds was a mouse. A lot of folks wouldn't hire a mouse even as a second engineering mate because of their size, but his résumé showed he was fresh out of school, just 19, but his tests looked solid. As long as the mouse was willing to work on a ship full of foxes, he'd do just fine. Most mice were fine around their natural predators, but some got skiddish around foxes and cats, just like she had a horrible time around bald eagles and other creatures that used to hunt red foxes.

She sent Jace a message telling him to hire the two, skipping the interviews unless he thought he needed to put his eyes on them. She needed engineering mates and didn't want to pull Benji into engineering for more than a few hours. And he wasn't the kit with an engineering head; that was Krissy, and she was too young to risk that close to the reactor.

She reached down and rubbed her belly. That last night with Jace before he left had been good. And it had apparently worked. She had taken a quick test this time to be sure. She'd also gone to the doctor that afternoon and confirmed the pregnancy. The doctor had then prescribed all the necessary supplements and medicines that a vixen in her late 30s needed when going through her first two trimesters of her fourth—she hoped—successful pregnancy in space would require. She'd program them into the ship's synthesizer as soon as she was on board, along with the other meds, including the ones that both Benji and Danny took each morning.

She wondered if she'd have another girl. In her way, Krissy was the easy child. But another boy might keep the Bartlett legacy alive. Not that Benji wouldn't have kits of his own with Trent or whoever he finally settled down with. But they might not be… they'd be her grandchild, and they would carry the Bartlett name. And Krissy would have kits, but they might bear another tod's name.

Somehow, she knew that Danny was like his Uncle Mark in that way as well. Those two were so much alike, even to the point of having the same sexuality, or asexuality. It had broken Mark's heart when she rejected him. She still loved him deeply. But she needed a tod fox who could love her fully, not just emotionally. It was Jason who could give her his heart and his body. Mark could have only given her his heart.

She knew Danny might someday give his heart to a wonderful male or female creature, but, like his uncle, his body was his.

Perhaps this little tod growing inside her… suddenly she was sure that it was a tod, a third son, would turn out to be like his father, or his grandfather, and be the fox who would pass on both the name and the genes.

CHAPTER 5

We were finally heading back to space. But that first meant taking a car to O'Hare. Early in the morning, Mommy got us all up.

Benji was crankier than usual. Something about Daddy calling him first thing in the morning and lecturing him, but not wanting to say anything more. He also smelled funny. Not like he did on mornings when he didn't take a shower, which was already—he would smell really strongly of tod fox if he didn't shower—but something else.

"Benji, you need to wash your sheets and night clothes." Mommy yelled as soon as he came out of his room. "They all have to be in the dryer before we leave, which is in less than an hour, so you'd better get them in the washer before you eat. See if Krissy or Danny has anything that should go with them."

"OK, Mom!"

I didn't know why Benji was so mad. He was usually happy to be going up to space. Maybe it had something to do with the fact that he wouldn't see Trent for six whole months. But he'd been texting Trent since before we got Earthside, so how would that change?

I ran back upstairs to get the bedding from my den, brought it to the laundry room, and handed it to Benji. His sheets smelled funny, like he did.

He grabbed my bedding from me. "Go downstairs and eat your breakfast kit!"

Benji never called me kit that way.

I went back downstairs and sat in my chair.

Mommy didn't have time to make anything special, so she was programming the synthesizer to make pre-made eggs and bacon. She set a plate in front of me, then looked upstairs. "Benjamin Bartholomew Bartlett, do not take your bad mood out on your brother!"

"Mom, you didn't need to spy on me. And telling Dad what I was doing, that was too much. He's threatening not to let me make 2D video calls from the ship when we're in port or at zero-g."

I stopped eating. Krissy looked up from her food. Something interesting was going on.

But Mommy just went upstairs to talk to Benji in person.

"Benji is in big trouble," Krissy said. "I bet it has to do with Trent."

I looked down at my synthesized eggs. "I bet it has to do with why he and his sheets smell funny."

After we were done eating, Benji put the laundry in the dryer, where it would sit for six months (something Mommy said had happened lots of times), and we headed out and got in the car. Benji helped put our four cases in the back.

In the car, I held my space bag carefully on my lap. Inside it was Mommy's special jar, with her sourdough mother in it. Mommy trusted me to keep it safe while we went back and forth between space and Earth. On the suborbital, it couldn't stay in my lap like it could everywhere else, so it had to go into my bag. But I kept my bag close and made sure it was upright until we got to the spaceport.

At the spaceport, Benji helped Mommy get the four big cases to the curb, then checked them all the way to Preston Station. He was being very helpful to Mommy instead of being all angry like he had been earlier. Mommy must have really told him off upstairs, even though she did it very quietly so Krissy and I couldn't hear.

We had to wait for a couple of hours before we could get on the suborbital that would take us to the spaceport at the base of Preston Station. The suborbital was like every other suborbital. They still only had lap belts, but at least they went high enough that they didn't shake as badly as airplanes.

In less than an hour, we were in the jungle around the base of the stalk. But the spaceport was air-conditioned inside. After walking off the docking tube from the suborbital, Mommy led us to the base of the stalk. We had reservations for a pod at 1300 local, which gave us an hour to wait.

Taking the pod to Preston Station felt like spending six hours in a hotel room. Our room on the pod was a family room for creatures the size of foxes, cats, rabbits, and the like. It had a head, complete with zero-g since we'd be in zero-g at the top of the stalk, some beds and couches, and big windows where we could look out and see Earth getting smaller and smaller as we went up.

As soon as we got into the room, Benji curled up on the bed, tail over his muzzle like Krissy and me, and started sleeping. I sat watching out the window, then picked up my tablet and started working. I had maths homework. I was already taking algebra, which Mommy said was quite advanced for nine. I'd start navigation math next, or maybe geometry, which was all about shapes and proving things. But I had a bunch of algebra problems to do, and I wanted to get some of them done before we had to head out. If I got my work done, I'd get a new assignment.

———

Mark looked at his tablet when he got into his room that afternoon.

To: MBartlett.resident@elgin_dundee.bors.ucgov

From: JBartlet@bartletfamilyfreight.co.space

Subject: Check these licenses

Mark, I hope asking you this won't get you into trouble. I need you to use your totally legitimate and legal skills at using the public access to the UC Space Licensing system, that I've never managed to confirm that the attached licenses are valid, and actually belong to the individuals who provided the license data and signatures to me. These are the three potential second officers I've actually received any nibbles from. But none of them smell quite right. Please do this quickly; we need to get into space ASAP.

Mark sighed. Jace was still relying on him to do the license checks.

He sent a quick message to his career services counselor, "Am I going to get into trouble running license checks for my brother?"

A couple of minutes later came the reply. "Come to the library, you can't run them from your tablet. I'll have to supervise."

He sighed and headed to the next building, where the career services library was located. His counselor, a hulking lioness named Nova Becker, had already logged one of the computer terminals into the system. He opened another window, pulled up his email, and began checking the licenses.

"You've done this before," Nova noted as he started processing the first license.

"Family freighters run on the margins. We tend to get a lot of guest crew who aren't qualified for the jobs they apply for. I've seen more forged licenses than legit. Yup—stolen number. This guy didn't even bother to make sure he got the right species."

He put the second one into the search and started running the checks. This one went further until it hit the checks for license status. "That is interesting, this license was issued a century ago. I didn't know one could get a 120-year licence."

Mark looked at the third one. "This one has to be fake. Skip King, putting your nickname on the license, that is a rookie mistake. He started running the checks. Everything kept going through. The checksums matched. The digital signatures matched. Even the issuing agent's signatures were right."

He looked at Nova. "Either this license is legit, or the forger is one of the best out there."

She looked at him. "What do you know about forgers?"

"I have seen my share of badly forged spacer licenses. Is that good enough?"

"Off the record."

"Is anything here off the record?"

"No, but you cannot be held liable for any crimes you admit to counseling staff, which includes career counseling."

"Maybe I've seen some well-done tax stamps, but nothing this good."

"I've never seen a forgery this good either. And I've worked with a few top forgers. They can be a challenge to find a new career for. You are easy, you know what you plan on doing, it is just making sure that you'll be able to do it without succumbing to temptation that will push you into breaking the law again."

Mark sighed and looked up at the lioness looking down at him. "I agree. But I can't see any better option."

"You won't be happy if you aren't helping your family. I don't see a better option either."

———

Daddy had the ship parked on the habitat ring of Preston Station. When we got off the pod at the station, we were in the hub at zero-g, but it was a quick trip down the spoke to the habitat ring.

Preston station is one of the biggest stations around Earth. Some folks said you could see it from the ground, but I never tried from New Chicago or Phoenix, even though both are close enough to north of it.

The ring is nearly 30 kilometers around, so the spokes are almost ten kilometers long. Unlike MarsPort, creatures don't dive down the spokes; they have to take cars, almost like little pods, except they don't take hours, only a few minutes.

It had been a long day, so I was glad to get to the ship.

"We're almost there, kits," Mommy told us when we got off the spoke elevator in the Blue Shopping Plaza. It was the nice one with the big Spacers Supply, almost as big as the one on Earth, and the food court that sometimes had real food.

She led us towards the garden with the big fountain that shot real water into the air, which was weird to watch since it didn't come down where it would on Earth.

Then we took another lift down to the lowest level until we found the right docking tube. Mommy had to use her minitablet comm to unlock the tube even though the sign above the tube said "Bartlett Family Freighter ENA-94252."

It was wonderful to be back on the ship. It smelled like home more than our Earthside home did.

When we got there, Daddy was on the rec deck talking to a big jack hare, bigger than I thought jack hares could get, and a tiny mouse.

"Reggie, kits, I'd like you to meet our engineering mates. This is Jax and Pete. Jax is the one with the big ears and the bum paw."

"Hiya, kits," Jax said. I could see Jax's left paw was… wrong. It looked like it had been smashed or something. But he didn't seem to mind.

Pete actually ran up Jax's jumpsuit and got onto Jax's shoulders to look at us. "Hey, glad to be working with you all for my first gig."

Mommy looked at them. "I need to stow the kits and talk to Jace for a bit, but if you two want to meet me in the galley at 1700… hang on, I'm still on home time." Mommy looked at her watch. "It's already 2000 ships time, but only 1400 for me and the kits. We may be off for a bit. You two up to meeting at 2300, or do you want to drag an old vixen out of her bunk at 0900 tomorrow and make her start shifting to ships time?"

I faked a big yawn. "Mommy, I think I'm going to head up to my den and go to bed."

"Not until you unpack your bags, you aren't, kitto. And that includes putting my sourdough mother in the galley."

"Mommy, where is my big bag?"

Daddy looked at us. "Your bags should be coming in through the cargo hold. It's open to the station so that they can load in atmosphere. Benji, come with me. We'll fetch them. Danny, take the sourdough mother up to the galley, and I'll get your bag up to you."

I climbed the ladder. It was shorter than when I climbed it the last time back in late October on the Moon. But it was weird climbing it at a bit over 1g at the bottom level of Preston Station. We never thrust more than 0.9g, so 1g was a bit more than I was used to.

I stopped in the galley and carefully removed the jar with Mommy's sourdough mother. Before I set it on the counter, I took off the lid and the cloth and took a deep sniff. It had this wonderful smell that was kind of like Mommy's bread, but even more. I then carefully put the cloth back on and put on the ring, but not the rest of the lid. I knew Mommy only used the rest of the lid when we were traveling. She didn't mind if I took a sniff. I'd seen her do it before she put some into the bread before letting it rise.

I then climbed up the stairs and found my den. I had to spend a lot of time getting all the pads and cushions just right. They always seemed to get into the wrong places during the winter.

"Danny, I have your case," Daddy called.

I climbed out of my den. Daddy had set my case in front of my den. He was busy unpacking Mommy's case into the lockers by their berth.

I spent an hour putting away my clothes and other things into the lockers around my den. At that point, I really was sleepy. I went into the head, and changed into my night clothes—pajamas that had silly cartoon rockets on them.

Mommy had come up the ladder and looked really tired, more tired than a day of travel usually made her.

"Mommy, Daddy, I'm going to go into my den and sleep."

Mommy leaned over and gave the top of my head a good-night lick.

Then Daddy picked me up and gave me a big, good-night hug, followed by a lick on my chin. "I'm not going to be able to lift you up before long, Danno. At least not when we're at 1g."

I trotted into my den, shut off the light, curled into a tiny ball, and was soon asleep, glad to be back on the ship, even if we weren't quite in space yet.

———

Even after the family arrived, it took two days to load the cargo.

Jason was frustrated because the second officer he'd contracted kept making excuses, delaying his boarding. First, the weather from wherever he lived in far northern North America—far enough north that his interview had to be voice only—had delayed his connection to the suborbital to Preston Spaceport. Then there was a glitch in his pod reservation, which pushed it so that his pod would arrive the day they were scheduled to launch. Finally, when he got to Preston, he texted saying he'd been given bad directions, had been sent to the far side of the habitat ring, and was having to wait for a train to get him around.

Fortunately, Benji, who was still desperate to make up for the incident in which he and Trent had been on an indecent video call, was willing to help with cargo loading supervision. Even at thirteen, or thirteen and a half, when Benji was trying to argue to say that what he had done wasn't that bad, he actually had a good head for cargo balancing. And this load had to be both carefully balanced and staged. Half the load consisted of machine parts to be delivered to Ceres Labs, while the other half was agricultural products for Mars, including nearly half a tonne of pig and cow embryos.

Jason was starting to get concerned that he would have to fly to Mars short-handed, which would have been barely legal. Between him and Regina, they had all the needed licenses to fly. And Jax was a fully certified engineer, so he could sit in the operating engineer's seat for docking at Mars, the one time the bridge actually needed two bodies.

Maybe that would be better. Reggie knew her limits, probably better than he did. But he worried about the new kit, perhaps even more than he would have if she hadn't miscarried less than a year earlier. He thought that maybe she and the unborn kit would get less radiation in the bridge than down in engineering.

He checked the newly installed crew/passenger position indication. The kits were all in their berths—dens for Krissy and Danny. Reggie, Jax, and Pete were all down in engineering, strapped in and ready to drop away from Preston.

Ramon was… where was that ferret? He looked around only to see the ferret strapped into the sensors station, a ferret-sized helmet on. He thought back and remembered that, even though he was their maintenance tech, he was also a licensed sensors operator.

They were less than five minutes away from drop, two minutes from when they would need to pull the docking tube from the station, when the station-side door comm buzzed.

Jason clicked the comms. The fox standing there was older than he expected. Skip King was much older than most spacers, in his sixties.

Few spacers make it past fifty, but Skip King looked to be in his mid-sixties and also in excellent shape.

He had a mottled coat, a mix of black and red across his head, and what Jason could see of his back and shoulders under the crisp jumpsuit.

Looking at that suit, Jason realized he could have lived that long and still fly. Skip King wasn't a spacer; he was a fleeter. Nothing in his résumé mentioned his Fleet career. His résumé had made him look much younger.

"Permission to come aboard, Captain."

"Granted," Jason replied over the coms while pressing the releases that would open all three doors. "And get up to the bridge. We're less than five minutes before sep, and I need my co-pilot."

The older fox was quicker than Jason expected and was soon up on the bridge. He glanced around. "Good afternoon, Captain, Chief." He then took his seat and strapped in, including fastening the crotch strap. That would have reminded Jason of Mark or Danny. Except he also knew that fleeters, or at least fleeters used to being in cockpits, also were very diligent about fastening all five points.

"Bartlett Family, Preston Control. We show ready for departure. Are you green, or do you need another go around?"

"Preston Control, we are green, ready for separation and departure."

"Bartlett Family, separation in 5...4...3..."

CHAPTER 6

was in my den working on my social studies. My eyes burned from trying to read all the confusing names from the second session of the UC Parliament. They still were using all their animal names, which had to be written out with weird characters, which made reading them even harder. When we dropped away from Preston Station, it was almost like MECO. One second, we were at 1g. The next zero-g.

I had made sure to use the toilet before we went to zero-g. I wasn't wearing my zero-g diapers. I was trying very hard not to need them this year. I was nine. Nine was too old to wear diapers, even at zero-g. But thinking about not wearing them was making me need to pee.

"Prepare for thrust in 5."

"Engineering bringing reactor to full."

I liked hearing Daddy and Mommy talking back and forth when we were getting ready for thrust. I could hold it for five minutes. I'd only just gone. I could hold it.

I uncurled and flew out of my den. I'd been thinking about it too hard, and now I couldn't hold it.

I flew right to the head. I pulled the handle and floated inside. I bounced off the far wall and then came to a stop at the cabinet. I pulled it open and found the small attachments. Daddy had put little packets of wipes that said "for use for zero-g attachment discomfort" on the outside, right in with my attachments. I grabbed one attachment and hooked it up to the hose, then I unzipped. I opened the packet and pulled out the wipe, and used it. Then I used the zero-g toilet. It still pulled, but it wasn't as bad. I couldn't feel it quite as much. It didn't hurt. I finished up, connected the hose to be cleaned, put the attachment into the cleaner, and everything else into the trash. I washed my paws and went back outside.

"Thrust in 10...9..."

I quickly pushed down to the floor and lay on my back. Mommy and Daddy told me that was what I had to do if I ever got caught somewhere other than my den or a seat when thrust hit.

"3...2...1...MARK."

The weight came up quickly. Once I could feel we were at speed, I pushed to my feet.

"We are secure and thrusting to Mars. 13 days until flip. Ship on autopilot."

I stood and watched the ladder to the bridge.

First, I saw Ramon come down. He wasn't on the bridge very often unless he was fixing things. But he had a sensor helmet in his paw. He must have been working sensors for Daddy.

Then Daddy came down. Another fox followed him I didn't recognize. His jumpsuit looked like it had been ironed. Nobody ironed their jumpsuits. He even had a name patch, which said "King."

Daddy looked at me. "Danny, this is Skip King, my co-pilot. I'm taking him down to meet the rest of the family and crew."

I followed them down the ladder to the rec deck.

Benji was unstrapping when we got there. Krissy followed us down from the lower berths.

We all waited until Mommy came up from Engineering with Jax and Pete.

Once Mommy was up the ladder, she looked at Daddy. "Engineering is secure, the reactor is running at 100%, flow to the engines is... Father, what in blazes are you doing here?!"

———

"Reggie, I've met your father face to face once, at our Earthside wedding reception nearly seventeen years ago."

Regina looked across their tiny berth at her husband. They had pulled the door shut and hoped that nobody could hear their... discussion.

"Since then, you've talked to him on 2D, or just audio, two, maybe three, times a year: his birthday, your birthday, and maybe the anniversary of your mom's death if we're not under thrust. I leave you alone for those calls because... because it is safer for both of us."

She looked at Jace. He meant well and... Father was Father. He'd probably manipulated the whole thing. For all she knew, he'd pulled strings or done something else to make sure he was the only creature who Jace could possibly hire.

"Jace, come on, Skip King, Kingsley Schroeder. I think Krissy could have figured that one out."

"That fooled more than half of the tods in your life."

"Mark knew?"

"I had him check the licenses of all three applicants. The other two were forgeries."

"I knew it. Father set you up. He knew we'd need a second officer, and he found a way to send in two obvious fakes and then his stellar real résumé done up just enough that you wouldn't notice it was for a decorated fleet officer, a retired cutter captain."

"I thought your father spent half his career at Fleet Station, West Africa, and retired from New Brussles at Fleet HQ."

"He earned his rocket and helmed a cutter for five years before they decided to make him spend years pushing paper without giving him a star. And don't you dare ask him about that. He loves the fleet, but he hates the politics that kept him from retiring as Admiral Schroeder."

Jason looked at her, his ears down and eyes wide. Damn it, how did foxes... how did Jason of all foxes learn that expression, the one that could disarm and melt even the hardest sentient heart? "We're stuck with him. So what do we do?"

Regina sighed. "We live with it. If Father went to all this trouble, it's probably because he wants to meet his grandkits. I've kept them from him. We should let him get to know them. I'm sure after six months they'll hate him as much as I do."

Jace laughed. "Do you think he'll be that bad. He's been retired for six years."

"Jason Bartholomew Bartlett, he ironed his spacer's jumpsuit and sewed a nametag on it. I'm sure every other jumpsuit he packed is identical."

Her tail wagged just a bit. "It might be good for Benji. Father is the best pilot trainer I've ever met. He did get me to pass my pilot's license test. If anyone can get Benji over his testing yips, it will be Father."

"And maybe he can figure out how to tell him why we're so upset about his little call."

"But Danny… He'll never understand Danny. I can't see Danny and the fleet."

Jace reached down and rubbed her belly. "Do we tell him about number four?"

"Not until we reach Ceres, at the earliest. I think we keep that to ourselves at least that long. I want to make sure he's safe. I have the extra medical equipment the doctor sent in my case, so you can do the scans she'll need. We'll need to transmit them when we're at zero-g."

"At least the new coms will let her send us back text results. You sure it's a he?"

"I was right the last three times, wasn't I?"

He started licking her belly.

"Jason, that is how we got into this mess."

"I thought you wanted number four. Besides, you can't carry two at once."

She reached up and shut off the berth's light.

———

The morning after we left Preston Station, I came down for breakfast.

Mommy was scrambling a big pan of eggs and frying a bunch of bacon. It was all from the food synthesizer, but cooking synthesized food was better than having the synthesizer make cooked food. She also had a big bowl sitting there, covered with a cloth, so she was baking two or maybe three loaves of bread.

But Mommy also looked a bit tired, and maybe a tiny bit sick. She'd been like this some mornings right after we left Mars the last time. Then she had a new kit that died before being born. I hoped that if she had another new kit inside, a new little brother or sister, this one wouldn't make Mommy sick and sad again, but would be born and become a living little brother and sister.

Krissy was sitting, eating a bowl of synthesized berries. She'd decided that eating berries was good for her fur, even with Mommy telling her eggs were better for her fur than berries. Krissy was still trying to be really girlish, which I thought was extra silly since she was as good at engineering as Mommy, and Mommy wasn't that girlish, other than being Mommy.

Daddy was working the food synthesizer, making tortillas, which weren't as bad as synthesized bread or toast, so they would be better with our eggs and bacon.

I climbed into my chair at the table and said, "Good morning."

Mommy looked over from the pan where she was stirring the eggs. "Good morning, Danny. How did you sleep?"

"Good. I'm glad to be back in space. I sleep better in real space— when we are flying."

Daddy looked at me. "I know what you mean, Kitto."

Benji came up the ladder carrying his tablet. "This is great, I can text Trent even when we are at thrust, and he can text me back. It's almost as good as when we were in Phoenix. But no 2D calls… not that I'm allowed those anyway." He then glared at Mommy and Daddy. He's been mad at them about that since we left Earth.

Daddy looked at him. "Don't use all of our bandwidth texting with Trent. We need some of that for actual business."

"Dad, a year ago, we were cut off when thrusting; now we get a lot. I mean, almost half a gigabit. It's just the lag that makes things like video not work. I can even download music, not that there is any good new music right now. All the new bands stink. AI Pop is all the rage, again. For like the thousandth time in the last few centuries. Haven't they learned that folks want real creatures making real music? Gees!"

"Sounds just like you at that age, Regina."

The co-pilot, who was apparently my Grandfather, had just come up the ladder and sat at the table.

"Father, did you even pay attention to my tastes in music when I was thirteen?" Mommy's ears were down. She looked a lot like Benji when he was mad at Mommy. "I thought you only cared that my quarters were ship-shape and that my claws were properly trimmed."

"Reggie, I was trying. Your mom was gone. When I was Earthside, I did my best."

"You still spent more time on ships than you did with your daughter. After your wife got sick from something that had no business killing a fox in the 4th century, and you took a few months of leave, then you left your eleven-year-old daughter to go back to your fleet career while a succession of nannies and governesses raised her. But when you did come for a short visit, oh, the house, her bedroom, and her had better be up to fleet standards."

"Reggie, I tried. I… If I'd taken a groundside position at that point, I'd never have advanced…"

"And how did that work out for you, Captain Schroeder?"

Daddy carried the pan of bacon over to the table. "I think breakfast is ready. We should eat up, and then the bridge crew needs to go topside and make sure this boat is still on course."

The rest of breakfast was very quiet.

———

King had always been Kingsley's nickname growing up and as a junior officer. He'd only started going by his full name when he made Lieutenant Commander and decided that it was proper to use his full name. That was about the time his daughter was born, and his career went on the fast track. The next two promotions came quickly, as did his first command, the cutter Franklin.

That was when things went sideways in King's life. Alexis got sick. Parvo. She should have had the vaccine; they all did. But the strain she caught was exotic. Reggie was at camp, and he was in space, so they both avoided it. But Alexis missed the symptoms until it was too late.

By the time she went to the doctor, they sent her to the base hospital to treat it, but other infections set in.

Alexis was dead before he could reach Earth. Reggie had to bury her mother's remains without her father at her side. And that was the start of the break between them—not that they had ever been as close as he wanted.

Now, he'd hoped to make up for it. He was trying, God, he was trying. But she wasn't going to make it easy, not that she'd made anything easy for him over the last 28 years.

After performing the routine, but a technically necessary daily check on the autopilot with Jason, King headed down, leaving his son-in-law to perform the other tasks that the ship's commander needed to perform in the bridge.

When he reached the access deck—the rec deck, as the family called it—he found both his grandsons there. Danny, the younger one, was working on the resistance trainer. His tail gave a little wag as he saw the nine-year-old being diligent with his conditioning. It was important for spacers and fleeters of all ages to keep their muscles and bones in shape when in unusual gravity. 0.9g was close to 1g, but was still a bit light. Spending some time with resistance training at the right resistance was one of the best things a spacer of any age could do to keep bones, muscles, and joints in shape.

He walked over to Benji, his older grandson. He had his tablet out. At breakfast, he'd been exchanging text messages with his paramour, a young tod fox named Trent, if King's surreptitious glances were accurate. First love was good for a young tod. Sometimes it lasted.

He'd met Alexis when he was about Benji's age. Actually, he'd known Alexis since they were tiny kits. They grew up in the same building in Berlin. He lived on the fifth floor, and she lived on the third. But when they were in their teens, they found they were a bit more than friends and neighbors. She waited while he went to the Fleet Academy, and they were married after he completed his first posting on the Sparrow—the original Sparrow, not the one currently flying that had been involved in the recent incident.

"What are you working on, Ben?"

"It's Benji, Grandfather?"

"Call me King. Grandfather sounds so... old."

"OK. I'm... I'm reviewing the questions for the co-pilot's exam. I have these down. It's the stick test. I'm on the simulator until I load up the sample test program, then I crash. I can perform a simulated mid-course flip and a zero-g dock every time if I just run the program, but not when it is a test."

King laughed. "Kit, you get the test yips. I've known more pilots to get them than I could count. It runs in the family. Reggie, your mom, got them something fierce when she first went for her co-pilot test. And King Schroeder nearly failed out of the Fleet Academy because he'd get test yips so bad when it came to practicals."

"What do you do about them?"

"You forget that it's a test. You don't treat it any differently than any other run on a simulator, and when it comes to your pilot's test, you treat it like any other flight."

King walked over to the simulator, which sat in a corner of the rec deck main room. He turned it on and loaded a program without telling Benji which one. "Come on, Benjamin Bartlett, show me what you've got."

Benji hopped up and strapped himself into the sim. Like most spacers and too many fleeters, he just fastened the shoulder and waist straps, only four points. But that wasn't anything that would cause him to fail a civilian test. Even the fleet lets cadets pass with that one these days.

He then put his right paw on the stick and tapped the start button with his left foot. The mid-course flip scenario loaded. King watched as the teenage kit tapped the MECO signal with his left paw, then noted that once the sim reported MECO, he tapped the stick to perform the delicate dance of flipping the ship 180 degrees around to point the main engines back the other way, then tapped the button to signal Engineering to throttle back up.

When the sim paused and brought up the score of 98%, Benji's tail started wagging, and he looked at King. "That was a sample test?"

"It seemed nice, and didn't throw any complications at you. The co-pilot tests only get complications about half the time. If your flip is complication-free, expect them on your dock. And if you get complications on the flip, your dock should be clean."

"But that was just like any other sim."

King looked at his grandson. "The tests are just another sim. That is what you need to remember. Now let's see how you do docking. Then I'm going to make you do it again. It might be a test load or just practice."

"Thank you, King."

"And while you are at it, tell me about this young tod that has my grandson all distracted."

CHAPTER 7

was working on the resistance trainer down on the rec deck. Uncle Mark had told me that it was important, even for a small kit, to use it every day. Even with Uncle Mark stuck on Earth, probably forever, I didn't want to disappoint him. Three sets of bench presses, three sets of pull-downs, three sets of leg presses, three sets of curls with each limb, and then the tail curls. The tail curls always made me laugh. Putting a strap around my tail and wagging it slowly back and forth seemed silly, but Uncle Mark said that even our tails had to keep strong; otherwise, how would we be able to wag them properly when we were happy?

Skip King, the fox who was apparently my grandfather, Mommy's dad, came down the ladder and started talking to Benji. Then he and Benji went over to the simulator. I got this funny feeling in my stomach. Not like being sick, but… I don't know. It was like I wanted him to pay attention to me. This old fox was a stranger. And he and Mommy had a big fight at breakfast. He made Mommy really mad, and I was sure she had my little brother or sister inside, and it was because of Uncle Mark fucking (I shouldn't use that word) up that my last little brother or sister died and wasn't born. I didn't want to like this old fox.

But he was making Benji happy. Benji's tail was wagging for the first time since we left our Earthside house. And that made me happy. Benji could be mean to me, but he was my big brother, and that made him important to me. I loved him. Not like I loved Mommy and Daddy, or had loved Grandpa, who I still missed—even if I hated his stinky cigarettes. But I knew I loved Krissy and Benji in their way.

When I was done with my tail curls, Benji and Skip King, Grandfather, King, as he told Benji to call him, were still working on the simulator. I went upstairs to my den, got my tablet, then came down to the galley and sat at the table to work on my Social Studies.

"Explain the key decisions made by the second and third sessions of the UC Parliament held between 97 and 104 PC."

I looked at the question. I'd tried to read the part about the second and third sessions of Parliament. But they had all the weird animal names because half the members hadn't adopted human names yet. That made the words jump around even more.

I knew when I read, I could remember what I read, but only if I didn't get the words all mixed up. That was why I liked listening to what I read, but my social studies book didn't have an audio version. And it wouldn't load into the book reader.

I grabbed the chapter again and tried to load it. "Error, this book is locked against audio conversion," the reader said.

I thought about saying the dirty word that Uncle Mark had taught me.

Daddy was up on the bridge working. Mommy was down in Engineering. On the first flight with new engineering mates, she always had to spend more time down there. Krissy was in her den working on her own homework.

King came up the ladder with a zero-g mug.

"Hey, Dan…"

"It's Danny, King."

"OK, Danny."

He got a funny look on his face before walking over to the synthesizer and putting the mug in. I smelled it start pouring more coffee.

"You want any coffee, Danny?"

"Mommy doesn't let me drink coffee."

"A little coffee never hurt a kit." He pulled his mug out, then got another mug from the cabinet, and stuck it in the synthesizer. "I'll have yours made with lots of milk and sugar."

He then handed it to me and sat down next to me.

"So, what are you working on?"

"Social studies. I'm having trouble with the chapter on the second and third sessions of the parliament. The chapter is hard to read with all the animal names."

"Try reading it to me."

"I can't read it out loud any better than I can read it quietly. The words get all mixed up."

I picked up the mug of coffee and took a sip. It was bitter and... it wasn't as yucky as I thought it would be. The milk and sugar made it kind of sweet and creamy. And it did make my head a bit clearer and help my thoughts not race as much, kind of like the medicine Mommy gave me in the morning.

"Show me."

I started reading. But I hardly got two screens in before I got all confused between the animal names and the big words. I started saying words I knew all wrong, and then I started crying.

King stood up, his ears flat. "I didn't know you were a big crybaby." He then stomped down the ladder.

I was still crying when Mommy came up to start making lunch.

"Danny, honey, what is the matter?"

"I was working on social studies. I can't understand it 'cus I can't read it. King, Grandfather, came in and told me to read it to him, but when I got all confused, I started crying. He called me a crybaby and went downstairs."

Mommy's ears went flat. She kissed me. "Danny, I'll read your social studies for you after lunch. Why don't you go up to your den and watch something fun for a bit? I'll bring you a sandwich up there. Take your drink... wait a second, did he give you a mug of coffee... take it with you. The damage is probably already done. You're half a Schroeder."

I headed up to my den with my tablet and my zero-g mug of coffee. I was glad Mommy was mad at King for calling me a crybaby.

In my den, I found a bunch of silly videos about the rabbit, which looked more like a hare, and the funny-talking hunter, and I started watching them. The silly videos helped, but I still sat there, having to stroke my tail really fast and hard to feel better.

———

Ramon came out of his berth. The first trip was always quiet, sometimes too quiet. He had fixed nearly everything that the crews that had worked on the ship performing winter upgrades had broken, and nothing else had a chance to break yet. He'd been spending more time in his berth looking at other possible tweaks and improvements he could make to the ship to make his family more comfortable.

He wasn't sure at what point the Bartletts had moved from being his employers to his crew to his family. It just happened, like his decision that he was never leaving this ship other than for medical checkups, to get supplies that he couldn't trust ordering, and when he ejected his body into space after the inevitable spacers got too bad.

He had been trying to figure out how best to run the sensors bundle from the bridge down to Danny's berth—den, as the young fox called it. He had already finished installing all of the electronics into the new sensor helmet that would fit the fox kit for at least the next three or four years, unless he grew faster than most kits. But there were dozens of wires and fibers that would need to be routed between the bridge and the upper berthing deck, and the conduits between those decks were already tight, and he didn't want to cut off the ones he used to get around.

"Good afternoon, Chief."

He froze. The fox, Skip King, according to his official registration as guest crew, but now everyone knew he was actually Captain Kingsley Schroeder (retired) of the UC Fleet, was looking at him.

Heat rose in Ramon, a mix of anger and shame. "It was Fleeter Third Class, Captain."

The fox's ears went flat. "Chief Ramon DeSantos, you earned every one of those stripes that I can still see on that old duty jumpsuit you still wear. As far as Admiral Crocker was concerned, you should have had a medal pinned to your chest, and every one of them restored."

Ramon looked at the floor. "I should have had a needle stuck in my arm and been sent to the long sleep. I nearly lost a code book. Admiral Crocker only let me go because of his daughter."

"Crock was an old friend of mine. I was at Fleet Station at the time, Chief. I knew exactly how he was feeling. My daughter was grown, and all but lost to me, and then his teenage daughter got kidnapped by a pirate. He would have given anything to get her back, then a damn fool ferret Chief risked his life to win her in a poker game."

The old fox put his paw on Ramon's shoulder. "If Nightingale's captain hadn't busted you down, you would have been discharged as a Chief. So as far as I'm concerned, Chief, you still hold the rank of Chief, and that is what I'm going to call you, whether you like it or not."

———

A few days into our flight, Ramon knocked on my den. "Danny, I have something for you."

I climbed out. Our ferret maintenance tech was standing there, wagging his tiny tail like he was a canine.

"Ramon, you've been living with foxes too long."

He stopped wagging his tail. Then he handed me a sensor helmet. It was my size, not like the big sensor helmet that Daddy and Uncle Mark used.

He also pointed to a new jack right next to my den. "I also put a sensor jack right here. You can plug into the sensors in your den. You don't have to go up to the bridge. You can control your sensors from your tablet."

I ran over and gave him a big hug. "Thank you, Ramon."

"Just looking out for my crew."

I looked at him. "Why does King call you Chief?"

"I was a Chief Petty Officer, once. Then I messed up. I messed up bad kit. I messed up worse than your uncle, but your grandfather doesn't see it that way. He thinks I'm a hero. I came close to being executed for what I did."

Ramon dropped the sensor helmet and walked away. He went into one of the maintenance hatches.

I was shaking. I didn't know why he told me that. I knew I shouldn't have asked.

I picked up the sensor helmet, plugged it into the jack, crawled into my den, and slipped it on. I was in my favorite place. I was the ship. Able to experience space from outside, see space without the ship's windows. Feel the tiny micrometeors fly by as they tickled my whiskers. I spent half the afternoon with the sensors helmet on.

That evening, I felt happier than I had in a long time when I went down to supper. I still needed help with my reading and social studies. I still didn't know why King was so mean to Mommy and to me, but we had time to figure it out.

————

Ramon woke in his berth. His heart was pounding. The berth stank.

Ferrets can use their scent glands defensively, as skunks do. They can't spray, but they can release a lot of foul musk when needed, and Ramon must have dumped both glands during his nightmare.

Ramon had lots of nightmares over the last seven years. But most were concerned about what he saw on the Cunningham ship. Not with Vesta afterwards. And his nightmare had never included him turning over the wrong card, his arrest, his… he died in his dream, executed, given the shot that leads to the forever sleep. Folks say if you die in your dream, you die in life, but he was alive. Alive, terrified, and with a bed that smelled of scared mustilid.

He sat up. He'd have to take his laundry, his bedding, and his clothing to the washer on the galley deck.

He checked his tablet; it was 0200. The Bartletts would be asleep. King, Captain Kingsley Schroder might not be. Retired Fleet captains were unknown to the dishonored Fleeter Second Class, especially those who tried to insist that he should be respected as a Chief for the worst decision he ever made.

Ramon stripped out of his old duty uniform and his underwear, gathered it up with his bedding, and tossed it all on the floor. He fumbled with a pair of clean underwear, then grabbed his other old duty uniform, but it was dirty too. Damn it. He'd have to put on one of the other things he had.

He looked in the small wardrobe. A few other things were hanging there. He wasn't going to put on the green jumpsuit. He never understood why they gave him that when he was discharged. But wandering around in a green jumpsuit with "PRISONER" written across the front and back in bright yellow might not sit well with the Bartletts, especially the kits.

He grabbed an actual spacer's jumpsuit in light blue that he'd picked up at Spacers Supply the last time he'd gone onto an actual space station a year or two ago. He had never worn it, preferring his old, worn, duty uniforms with all their patches and insignia removed. As he slipped it on, he noticed the fancy silk clothing hanging next to it.

He thought again about how close it had come if that ace hadn't come up, how at least two lives would have been lost. He would have died, sent off to the long sleep, just like in the nightmare he woke from. But he also knew that Rio Young would have murdered Daisy for her attempt at escape. He'd seen the look of murder in his eyes when he bet her.

As he brushed his paw along the silk shirt, he felt the pocket. He reached in and pulled out a single card, a 2 of clubs.

Ramon DeSantos never cheated at cards. He never needed to. That didn't mean that the same quick paws that could fix anything on a spaceship didn't know how to swap a card during a turn over. He still couldn't remember what had prompted him to paw the ace three hands earlier and then call for a fresh deck. It had to be fate. Just like how the other two aces were spades and hearts, so the ace of diamonds in his pocket was one he could use when his life and Daisy Crocket's life depended on it.

He slipped the card back into the pocket of the silk shirt. That card, like that shirt, belonged to a different creature, one who was born and died there on Vesta. Now he was simply Ramon, the mechanic on the Bartletts' freighter.

CHAPTER 8

I sat on the floor in the middle of the upper berthing deck with my tablet. It was the only safe place to sit to work on my social studies test. The rules said that if my tablet connected to another computer or detected another computer, I'd fail for cheating. The ship was full of computers. I couldn't use anything during the two hours I was taking the test but the test program and the social studies book. I couldn't copy any content from the book into the test. I could only copy names. Even before I sat down, I was already unhappy.

The test had a big question and a few little questions. The big question was "Write a six-paragraph essay about the important accomplishments of one member of the UC Parliament of your species (red fox) from the first six sessions (70-137). The first paragraph must be a thesis statement, followed by four paragraphs to develop your thesis, and one paragraph of conclusion."

When I read that, my heart started pounding. That was a lot of writing.

At least I put the keyboard on my tablet. I could write more easily on the keyboard than on the tablet. I didn't know how Benji sent all the texts to Trent that he did it using just the tablet's keyboard.

As I worked on the test, it got harder. I couldn't spell a lot of the words I wanted to use. I couldn't go to other places to find them either. The test's spell check didn't help. I'd try and try to fix them and finally have to find other ways to say what I wanted.

I was still working on the last paragraph of the essay when the bar at the top started blinking, telling me I had less than a minute to finish. My heart started really beating hard. I started panting like I'd been running a lot. I managed to finish just before the timer reached zero.

Two days later, I came down to the galley while Mommy was putting bread into the oven for dinner.

"Mommy." My eyes stung, but I was blinking hard, trying not to cry. "I only got a C- on my social studies test. I worked so hard. I really tried. I don't think the teacher likes me. She said mean things. She said 'spell words the same way,' and 'wrong word.' She gave me a D on my long essay and told me I needed to 'write better.'"

Mommy took my tablet from my paw so hard that it almost hurt. Her ears were flat, and her tail was big, all bushed up.

Her eyes got big as she read all the mean things.

"The test wouldn't let me say the essay like they used to. I had to type it all out." I was starting to cry. I didn't want to cry over a test, but it was hard. "The spell check didn't have half the words I wanted to use. Even if the word was in the book, sometimes I'd spell it wrong and have to fix it. I couldn't copy except the funny names."

Mommy looked at me. "Danny, take a seat."

I hopped into my chair at the table.

Mommy walked over to the synthesizer and made us each a big cup of warm milk with a bit of fox-safe cocoa. Foxes can't have real chocolate, but the synthesizer can make something that tastes almost like it.

"Danny, I was supposed to take you down to Cambera over the winter. You remember the tests I had you take last year?"

"Yes, all the special reading out loud and the other things."

"The school in Cambera wanted to do more of those. They think you have a form of dyslexia. It makes it hard for you to read and spell. If they give you an official diagnosis, the school will let you use readers and text-to-speech, even now that you are old enough that most students can't use those anymore."

"Regina, the kit doesn't need to be coddled."

I looked up. King had just come down into the galley, his zero-g coffee mug in his paw.

"You struggled a bit, but then got straight and did fine. At least until you decided that you weren't going to finish up at the Fleet Academy, and were going to run off and become a civilian spacer with a couple of ratty spacer kits instead."

"Father, I was only able to learn to work around my dyslexia because of a couple of understanding teachers who helped me learn some tricks, even though my stubborn father wouldn't let me get officially diagnosed, even after nearly failing out of my third year of primary school."

Mommy stood and walked over so she was standing nose to nose with King. Her ears were totally flat. "You knew Mom her entire life. Did you know she couldn't read? Did you know she used cunning and trickery to get through school? Or were you one of the students who helped her?"

Mommy stomped to the other side of the galley, then stomped back. "Of course not. Even before he went to the academy, King Schroeder was probably too honorable to help his best friend and girlfriend cheat."

She sat on the table. Mommy never sits on the table.

"I think she died because she couldn't read. The medical office at West Africa Base had all these written forms online that had to be filled out for anything other than an emergency. When you were in space, which was all the fucking time, Mom had me help her fill them out, even at nine, ten, eleven. When she caught parvo, I was at that summer camp in Northern Europe you insisted I go to."

"Honey, I…"

"She didn't go to the hospital until she was sick enough to have a neighbor call for an ambulance. By then, she was so weak that… They flew me home from camp so that I could sit by her side and watch her die. But you were still in space and couldn't get home for nearly a month. I had to bury her. I had to sit in base housing with the base child advocate stopping by a few times every day to make sure I was eating and not burning the place down…"

She stood up and walked over to King. "Father, Danny will get the help he needs. I'm going to send a message to that school you made me use for my kits, or at least the first three, and see if there is a testing center on Mars that they will accept instead of doing the tests at their center in Cambera. And then I am going to send a very long email to Danny's social studies teacher and tell her to… I'll give her a piece of my mind. And if I happen to use some spacer's language instead of fleet language, so be it."

She then looked at me. "Danny, why don't you go up to your den, or somewhere where you can enjoy yourself. Don't think about homework for a few days. OK, honey?"

———

Regina looked down at the email. It wasn't as mean as the first three drafts. The first one was so full of spacer's language that she couldn't even think of sending it. The second one was probably as much a result of pregnancy hormones as her indignation over what she hoped was a certified teacher's misunderstanding or misinterpretation. The third one was, at least she thought, polite enough, but still honest and firm. It informed the teacher that Danny was at least the third generation in his family to struggle with reading, spelling, and related issues. She didn't detail the whole family history.

She reflected on what she'd learned about how generations of learning science from the human era got pushed aside for nearly three centuries by the arrogance of every other species and the multi-species education establishment that rose after the Sentience Wars and the formation of the UC.

At times, she almost wondered if the humanists weren't partially right. Humans weren't meant to be in charge, but they were meant to be the examples for every other sentient creature, or at least every other terrestrial sentient creature if there were any other sentient beings in the universe. By whatever means foxes, wolves, cats, deer, horses, ferrets, and the rest became sentient, their sentience came with all of the same strengths and weaknesses that had existed in human intelligence for millennia.

She read through the email and ran it through a strong spelling and grammar checker. If that teacher was going to complain about Danny's spelling and word use, she was going to make damned sure that she had spelled every word the same way. She was going to make sure that there were no obvious grammar errors and that she had used the correct word, and hadn't put any homophones or similar words in.

Then she sent a message to Jace on the bridge. "Jace, can you drop down here and proofread an email I need to send to one of Danny's teachers?"

She glanced at the clock and dashed out of her berth. Her bread was close to burning. That wouldn't do. Having to serve synthesized bread with supper would be something she'd be embarrassed about that night

As she climbed down the ladder, she tried to think about what to do about her father. He'd gotten Benji over his yips. He was going to be able to pass his co-pilot's exam when they got to Mars. That was pretty much a given.

But Father was upsetting things on the ship. Danny was… after today, she was sure Danny wouldn't want to be around him. He already seemed to be avoiding Father, and now he'd witnessed her fighting with him.

And she'd heard Ramon doing laundry in the middle of the night, and her pregnancy-sensitized senses told her why. She didn't know what set the ferret off in the middle of the night, but something told her whatever gave him a nightmare and suddenly had the ferret maintenance tech wearing a new spacer's jumpsuit instead of one of his worn fleet duty uniforms had to do with her father's insistence on calling him Chief instead of Ramon. She thought she might finally have to give in and hack into fleet records to get to the bottom of who Ramon DeSantos actually was—or maybe just call in a few of the favors fleeters owed her.

Either way, Kingsley Schroder, a.k.a. Skip King, was off her ship once they got to Mars. She might only be the first officer on the record. But if she told Jace that he was off the boat, he was off the boat. If that meant that she never had to talk to her father again, maybe that was for the better.

———

I looked at my tablet. It was an article from *Child Spacers*. I actually had it read out loud to make sure I wasn't misreading it. Sometimes when words get all mixed up, I think I'm reading something that isn't right.

"The United Creatures Space Regulation Authority will begin issuing Junior Operator Licenses on May 1st, 367 Earth Reckoning." It was what I thought I'd read. "These licences will include Sensor Operators, Engineering Monitoring Assistant, and Pilot Aide. Junior Operators must be at least 9 Earth years old or 5 Martian years old and will have to pass a written or oral exam and a practical exam. Junior operators will be able to perform shipboard operations under the supervision of a fully licensed operator, even if that operator is working another role, for up to four hours in a given day, provided that they are maintaining their schooling and other requirements, as is the case with any juvenile holding a full operating license."

I flew out of my den so fast it was almost like we were at zero-g, not 0.9g. Mommy and Daddy were both down in the galley having coffee after breakfast.

"Mommy, Daddy, it will be May when we get to Mars, right?"

"Yes, Kitto," Mommy replied.

"I want to take my Junior Sensors Operator's test when we get there. I'll take it when Benji takes his co-pilot's test."

Daddy looked at me. "What are you talking about, Danny?"

I handed him my tablet.

He read it, his ears going up, and then handed it to Mommy, whose tail started wagging.

"Danny, if you are going to take that test, you'd better make sure you can pass the oral exam," Mommy said.

"Mommy, why would the dentist need to examine me for a sensors test? I don't use my mouth for the sensors."

Mommy laughed. "An oral exam is like a written exam, except you get to answer the questions to the examiner instead of writing them on the computer."

My tail started wagging. "I won't have to write them out?"

"The spacer's exams have always had that option. I didn't take the written option for my co-pilot's exam." She got down on a knee so she could look me in the eye. "Danny, you know I have the same trouble reading as you do, don't you?"

"That was part of what you were fighting about with King the other day, wasn't it. You said your Mom couldn't read. She had the same trouble, too, didn't she?"

"Yes, and your grandfather doesn't really understand—even with the vixen he loved a lot not being able to read. Mom hid it from him for years."

"You said she got sick because she couldn't read?"

"No, she got sick because of a bad sickness. You know the parvo shot you get every year."

"Yes?" I hated getting shots, but Mommy said they kept me from getting sick. I had to get parvo and flu shots every year, and some others too, but not as often.

"She got a kind of parvo that the shots didn't cover. And it made her very sick. But she didn't go to the doctor because she'd have to read and write to get an appointment."

"Why didn't she just go to the doctor like we do on Earth, or at Luna Station, on Mars, or MarsPort?"

"Because West Africa Base, and most UC Bases don't work that way for family medical. Because the fleet is broken. Fleeters get good medical, but their families don't always."

"Is that why you hate the fleet?"

Daddy helped Mommy stand up and then sit in a chair. She usually could stand just fine.

Maybe it was the baby she was carrying, but hadn't told us about. I could smell that Mommy smelled different, kind of like she had on the way from Mars last year, but better.

"I don't hate the fleet, Danny. I didn't like being a fleet brat. And I realized I wouldn't like being a fleeter myself, but it was almost too late."

"What is bad about the fleet?"

"That is a long talk, Danny, and not for today. Today, you need to learn what is on the Junior Sensor Operator's test and start reviewing the questions. OK?"

My tail started wagging even harder. "OK. I'll go back to my den and look it up."

I turned to Daddy. "Daddy, that might use more of our new bandwidth. Will Benji get mad if I make his texts to Trent slower?"

"If he does, he can talk to me about it."

"OK."

———

"Benji, why don't you like being called Ben?"

Benji looked at the text from Trent. He had at least half an hour before any response to Trent would reach Earth. They'd gotten used to the lag, which was way worse than even if he were on Mars, but Trent still treated their conversations like texts, only sending one or two lines. Benji liked to send long emails full of emojis that helped him express how much he missed his best friend turned boyfriend.

He... he really wanted to try what he'd only done with his paw, and once sort of on that video call.

Oh, he now regretted that. Not because of how much trouble he got in for it. No, that was one of the things that made him glad King was on board, even if he was the only creature on the entire ship who seemed happy his grandfather was there.

"Benjamin Bartlett," King had explained only a few hours after he'd helped Benji start to realize that he didn't need to worry about his co-pilot's exam practical. "Creatures have thought that their video calls, 2D and 3D, were private for centuries. Most of the time, they were. But sometimes creatures they trust, their boyfriends, girlfriends, non-binary partners, whatever, have made recordings."

Benji looked at the older fox. "Trent would never..."

"I'm not saying that Trent made a recording, but it's happened millions of times over the last several centuries, OK."

"OK, King."

"And sometimes the connections aren't as secure as you think. Even the best privacy software and hardware isn't perfect."

He leaned in. "When I was at the academy, I... I did what you did, but with your grandmother, Alexis, so I guess it was a bit different since she was a vixen, and we were a few years older. But a few frames got captured due to a glitch in the Academy servers. They got shared. They were blurry, but..."

King pointed to his very distinctive coat, which was mottled red and black. "I'm like this even down there, Benji. When the video showed my paw down on... It wasn't much, just a really tight shot. First, I was really embarrassed when it started getting shared. Then."

King's ears went really flat. Not angry flat, embarrassed flat. "The academy found out who had been responsible for 'conduct that could discredit the fleet academy.' I had to spend two weeks working in the kitchen, serving three meals a day, cleaning the serving containers, and running with the large-animal Chiefs who conducted the academy's basic training. They run really fast up and down the steep hills on the edge of the academy grounds.

Benji then discovered that there were sick creatures who would have loved to have a copy of the videos of what he was doing. They would have thought videos of two thirteen-year-old fox kits doing what he and Trent were doing were... they would have... The videos would have been really illegal if they had existed.

He shook his head. He needed to respond to Trent so he could go back to studying. They were a few days from flip, and he needed to review the written part of the co-pilot's licence exam, and then he still had six more problems for his last Nav Maths One assignment before the final, which he wanted to take when they were at zero-g during the flip. If he took it then, he might get the result faster and could start Nav Maths Two and then start his actual navigator's training.

"Trent, something about Ben or even Benny isn't me. I'm Benji, that's all. It's my name. I'm not going to outgrow it. If you don't like having your boyfriend being named Benji, then... Your boyfriend is Benji, and he loves you. If you are going to break up with him over this when he's halfway to Mars, then I'm going to make sure everyone knows that you are the meanest fox, not only in all of New Chicago, but in all of North America, maybe on all of Earth. And I love you and miss you a lot. And I really want to..."

He deleted that last bit. That was too much, too close to what got him in trouble. He had thought about trying to describe what he wanted in text, but decided that was too much. He'd just have to imagine doing it with Trent when in his berth. He was going through a lot of extra underwear and was washing his paws a lot. But Mom hadn't complained about the laundry or the excess water usage, yet. Maybe she understood. Or maybe it was Dad who did.

CHAPTER 9

Daddy said we would be at zero-g for three hours during flip. Three hours was a long time right after lunch.

I should not have snuck down and had coffee, but it helped me study for my sensors exam and focus on my school work. I now had English and science, which had a lot of reading. Mommy told me not to have coffee, even after King gave me some. But it helped like the pill I took at breakfast, and sometimes if I didn't have some after lunch, my head would hurt.

"MECO in 5 minutes."

I was in my den reading my science. I put down my tablet and ran across to the bathroom. I had to make sure I peed before MECO. I really wanted not to have to pee in zero-g. This would only be three hours. I could make it three hours. Then I wouldn't have to use the zero-g toilet. Even with the wipes that made it hurt less, I still didn't like using it.

I got back into my den when Daddy started the countdown. "MECO in 5...4...3...2...1...MARK!"

When Mommy turned the engine off, I felt us go to zero-g. I was getting better at zero-g. It still made my tummy all flippy, but I didn't want to throw up.

I turned back to my science homework. It was all about Isaac Newton, a really old human, and his laws of motion. These were all things that any spacer knew. If I threw a ball, or if I kicked off a wall, it, or I, would keep moving without changing direction. The only creature I'd ever seen change direction without bouncing off a wall was Uncle Mark. He could do something with his tail and his body to change in mid-air. I never figured that out. If I tried, I just got spinning, and that often made me sick.

But there was a lot more of the science reading about Newton. I had to go back and read it a few times, because it wasn't letting me use the book reader, just like my social studies. This made me sad. Mommy said that maybe the testing center on Mars, not the one where I was going to get my Junior Sensors Operator licence, but the other one, would let me get the books read aloud again. But I had to struggle to read.

After I finally finished the reading, I had to pee. I knew I shouldn't have had the coffee. It always made me need to pee more than other things.

I looked at my watch. We wouldn't be thrusting again for another hour. Daddy and King had to do a lot of work to make sure we were where we were supposed to be, and then run a bunch of other checks to make sure we were pointed in the right direction to start flying to where Mars would be when we got there. That was one of the hard parts about navigation in space. Planets and asteroids moved while we were flying between them.

I couldn't hold my pee for a whole hour. I had to go, and go then. I put my tablet in its holder and headed across to the head. I had already waited too long, focusing on my reading. I'd let myself get too focused and forgot to listen to my body. Mommy says I can't do that, or I'd have an accident or forget to eat.

The head was empty when I got there, so I went inside and locked the door. I then quickly got the attachment and the wipes. I started hooking up the attachment, but it slipped from my paw. I said the bad word that Uncle Mark had taught me, out loud, really loud. I had to swim in the air to get to the floor to bounce off to get the attachment. Then I had dropped the wipe and the hose.

I had to make two more bounces to get them, and I was getting to where I was really going to have to go.

I finally got everything and hooked the attachment to the hose.

I unzipped my jumpsuit, got my, you know, out, and started wiping when… I peed. I peed right there in the air. It was an accident, but I'd waited too long. There was a big bubble of pee floating right there in the air, but lots of little bubbles of pee floating all over the head. Worse, one of them had drifted right into me and got my jumpsuit wet.

I grabbed the hose and started sucking the big bubble in, but that made it move, splashing me even more. Now I smelled of pee.

I started moving around, trying to suck up all the little bubbles, but they kept finding me.

Someone started pounding on the door. "Who's in there taking so long?"

It was King. I didn't want him, of all foxes, to see me in here with pee all over my jumpsuit and my private still hanging out.

I'd locked the door. I always lock the door. But I saw the lock turning. I still had to finish cleaning up. There were still bits of pee floating. I still had to clean myself. I still… I started crying.

The door opened. "What happened in here. Daniel, can't you use the zero-g yet, at your age? And you're crying again like a tiny crybaby."

He shot through the door of the head and grabbed me by the scruff. Mommy says nobody is to grab me by the scruff. That is almost as bad as touching my privates. But King just grabbed my scruff. He then dragged me through the rest of the pee, making my stinking jumpsuit stink even more.

"Put your dick back in your jumpsuit, and then I'll give you something to cry about, crybaby."

I fumbled to put my private back inside and zip my jumpsuit.

Then King pushed off out to the center of the deck. He tucked his footpaw into a foothold and pulled me down against his leg. He grabbed my tail in his teeth and, with the hand that wasn't holding my scruff, he started spanking me. It hurt. He hit me hard.

"Father, you put Danny down this instant."

Mommy had just come up the ladder. Her ears were flat, and her tail was bigger than I've ever seen.

"You are to stay in your berth until we dock at Marsport. That is the last straw. Someone will bring you your meals, and someone will let you out to go to the head. But if you talk to any of my children between now and when you get off this ship, I'll… I'll… I might just murder you and join my brother-in-law in rehab."

———

Jason looked at Regina across their small berth. "Are you going to report your father to the authorities? That was child abuse."

His wife looked back at him. "I… I don't know. Maybe he needs to go to rehab. But if he gets arrested on Mars."

Jason shuddered. "Nobody deserves Martian prisons." He looked at the door to their berth and confirmed it was shut.

"Reggie, you don't have a clue how bad they are."

"You've told me."

"No, I… I haven't. I told you about the boredom, I told you about the despair, the stink, the fear, the gangs. I never told you about my cellmate."

"You said he was a big cat, a Maine Coon. Bigger than you, rare for a cat."

"I never told you what he did… at least seven times I can remember. He had a girlfriend on the outside, but it didn't matter. Starting on my first night, he…"

Regina pulled him into a hug. "Jace, you don't have to tell me. You've had more nightmares than you know. I don't think you know how many nights you've quivered and shaken in your sleep, how many times I've held you tight when you were sleeping, how many of my sleepless nights have been because I was holding my husband like he was a tiny scared kit who didn't even realize that he was having a nightmare."

Jason looked at her. He loved her even more than he had for almost eighteen years at that moment. "You never said anything. Why?"

"I figured you'd tell me when you were ready. I also knew you saw a counselor for a year after that. You pretended that you were getting… what was it, skiing lessons? Like the fox, who gets cold if we don't keep our winter home above 18 degrees, would ever go skiing."

"There is water skiing. That is a warm-weather activity."

"Our Earthside home is in the northern hemisphere, and we're Earthside during its winter."

He leaned back. "I'm sorry I let Kingsley fool me into bringing him aboard."

"It wasn't your fault. He manipulated things to get here. He's still the same fox who thinks he runs everything, and everything and everyone should follow his orders."

Jace suddenly realized that in a week and a half, the ship would be at Mars. "How am I going to dock without a co-pilot?"

"Bend the rules. Your apprentice co-pilot can watch the gauges and have your backup sensors operator on sensors."

"You want me to put both uncertified kits on the bridge?"

"No, you dopey fox. Put Benji in the co-pilot's seat, where he'll be once he is certified, and put Ramon on sensors. He's fully certified, and with him there, you'll still have two licenses on the bridge."

"But I won't have two creatures licensed to touch the stick. If something happens…"

"You yell, and I can get up there from engineering in less than a minute, even pregnant."

Regina looked at him. "We're going to have to move up that timeline, too. Danny's figured it out."

"How has our youngest, who has never seen you pregnant, figured it out?"

"First of all, Danny has the best nose on the ship. Second, Danny had smelled me pregnant last year, before I miscarried. He's smart enough to have figured it out. I've seen the way he's looked at me. He knows, he's just not saying anything to me because we haven't said anything to him."

"Are we OK? The scan we did just before flip?"

"My OB on Earth said everything looks good. She also confirmed what I already knew."

"I'm… we're having a third boy?"

"Krissy and I are about to be seriously outnumbered, especially if Benji drags Trent up with us next year."

"They'll be 14, do you really think…"

"I don't know. But Trent's parents live on a basic income. And he doesn't strike me as the sort to want that lifestyle, even before he and Benji decided they were more than friends."

Jason laughed. "I think I'd rather have my son's teenage boyfriend than my wife's estranged father, even if he's just more cargo I'm carrying."

Regina looked at him. "That reminds me. I need to let Ramon know that it is time to take King for his walk."

"Is it really a good idea to have Ramon be the one who escorts your father to the head?"

"Right now, I think the only one on this boat that is madder at King Schroder than me, or possibly Danny, is Ramon. My father tore open some wounds on our best crew member that should never have been touched. Benji says that Ramon has been crying at night. Ramon is crying again. He hasn't done that since he first came aboard. I even had to sneak in there and take his shot."

Jason looked at her. "Do you think he even knows that we know he has an illegally obtained euthanasia shot?"

"No, I don't think he does. Nor does he know that I discovered why he was discharged and no longer a Chief Petty Officer."

Jason looked at her. "You aren't going to tell me, are you?"

"That is not for me to share. Just know that I now trust him more than I ever did before. But do not ever play cards with him. Not even a friendly game of go fishing."

I didn't want to come out of my den for three days after… After the accident in the head… After King hit me.

I stayed in there. Sometimes I watched a video. I spent a lot of time wearing the sensors helmet and practicing being on sensors. But a lot of the time, I just lay there in a tight ball. I was always stroking my tail.

I stroked it so much that it became really soft, and all the undercoat came out and was covering my den.

Mommy tried to convince me to come down for supper each night, promising he would not be there. But I didn't want to see Daddy, or Benji, or Krissy either. Jax and Pete were strangers, and Ramon hardly came to supper. For the first two days, she gave up and brought me supper. She brought me breakfast and lunch, too.

On the third day, Mommy sat outside my den. "Danny, why aren't you coming out?"

"I don't know, Mommy. I think I'm broken. I made your dad so mad that he hit me. He bit me, and he hit me, and he grabbed my scruff."

"Danny, my father was the one who was wrong. You did nothing wrong. You had an accident. You had coffee that day, didn't you?"

"Yes, Mommy."

"Who first told you to have coffee?"

"He did. But it does make me think better."

"No, your medicine does. If your medicine isn't helping enough, then we need to talk to the doctor."

"But she's on Earth; it will be months before we're on Earth. And she'll want a blood test. I don't like blood tests. They are worse than shots. They have to take blood. They really hurt."

"They only hurt because you won't hold still. I always tell you to hold still."

"But the needle in my arm like that hurts. I try to be brave, but it isn't just a little pinch, like they say. It's never a little pinch."

"Are you still studying for your sensors test?"

"Yes, and I'm using the sensors helmet that Ramon made me on the ship's 3D printer. I'm practicing, not just enjoying being the ship. And I'm studying. Even without being able to use the reader, I've gotten mostly As and Bs on my science homework. But it's been all about inertia, which any spacer knows."

"Are you going to come to supper. Your family misses you, even Benji and Krissy."

"OK."

I crawled out of my bunk. I had snuck out in the middle of the night and taken a bath with only 10 millimeters of water, so I was at least clean. I was in my cream jumpsuit, the one that Benji's boyfriend Trevor said looked good on me, and I had on my favorite Fourth Doctor T-shirt. So I decided I could join the family again.

"I made stew tonight, with synthesized rabbit."

"Did you tell Jax you used a synthesized rabbit?

Mommy laughed. "Jax is a hare. And it is synthesized, not real."

"So King is really locked in his berth?"

"Except when Ramon lets him out to use the head."

"Mommy, I don't like him. He's mean."

"I agree. He's mean."

———

King woke to the knocking on the outside of his berth door. All he had to do was sleep and realize how badly he'd messed this up. All he'd wanted was a chance to get to know his grandkits, and instead he'd made a hash of things, just like he had everything in his life, except his fleet career.

He slid out of the bunk, crossed the two steps to the door, and opened it.

Of course, it was the ferret. That was the only creature on the ship Regina would let see him. But he had a holster over his shoulder and around his waist. Chief—no Ramon DeSantos, he refused to acknowledge the rank he'd earned—was armed. He had two 1mm slug throwers, one holstered and one in his paw.

One round from either pistol could easily kill a red fox without doing any damage to the hull, or even much of the interior of the freighter. A 1mm was a large gun for a creature the size of a ferret, but not overly large. It was fleet standard issue, but not for maintenance. DeSantos had served on Nightingale. Every enlisted fleeter on that ship had been trained in arms. Every one of them had been fully qualified with small arms. The ferret's paw holding the gun was steady.

"Captain," Ramon began. "Do you know why I have guns? It's to keep my family safe from those who would harm them. A few months ago, my second officer had to shoot me with a dart because, in my fear,

I came close to mistaking the fleeters who were coming in to arrest him for pirates. He knew I might kill one or more of those fleeters before they killed me. Or I might have shot one of the kits to keep them from being savaged like the Cunningham kittens."

The ferret pulled the slide back and took the safety off the pistol. "I never expected the biggest danger to the kits, to the family, to walk in the airlock in the guise of Regina Bartlett's father, lying his way onto their, my, boat."

He then put the gun right against King's chest, right over his heart. "You have about 30 seconds, Captain Schroeder, to tell me why I shouldn't pull this trigger and put the next shot into my own brain after programming the lock to cycle both of our bodies out into the black?"

"Che… Ramon, do what you think you have to." King's heart was pounding. He had to do something. The ferret was calm, too calm. If he didn't diffuse this, they were both dead.

"But I don't think you are a killer. You risked your life to save Daisy Crocker. You might not have been totally in your right mind, but you… part of you had to know what you were doing, or you wouldn't have risked what you did. You…"

Suddenly, something occurred to King, something impossible, but he knew it was true.

"You cheated. For the first time in your life, you cheated that night. You didn't win her. You…"

Ramon lowered the gun. "I'd palmed an ace a few hands earlier. When I saw the duce, I swapped it in as quickly as I could. Rio had the dead man's hand, but I was the dead man."

He put the gun into the holster and started walking towards the head, pointing King that way.

"Did you know that the drugs the fleet uses once a century or less to execute their criminals are the same that you can get if you are sick enough and beg to be euthanized. You can even get them to use them later. They have a long shelf life. Put them in a vein like the medicos do, and the long sleep comes in a second or less, and then everything just shuts down. Put them in a muscle for self-administration, it gives you about a minute before you go to sleep. When my spacers get so bad that I can't fix this ship anymore, probably when Benji is its captain, the way things look, I'll put myself in the lock some night, stick myself with a dose, and have the lock cycle itself. But that won't be for a decade or two."

He looked at King. "I have my shot in my quarters, if you want it. Or I can give you one of my guns. It might be better than going back to Earth. Your daughter is going to tell them what you did to Danny. The decorated Captain Kingsley Schroder is going to have a record for child abuse."

King walked into the head, took care of his business, and walked out.

The ferret was quiet as he led him back to his berth.

He spent a few hours thinking about what Ramon had to say. He… no, he wasn't going to kill himself. He was going to do better. He needed to fix things, fix himself. When he got back to Earth, he'd get help. He'd figure out why he was… wrong. And then he'd try again. If not with Regina and Jason, maybe Benji and his boy, or whatever boy he settled with. Benji seemed to like him. King wasn't that old. And because he was a fleeter where the shielding had been better even years ago, he wasn't as likely as Jason and Regina to suffer the effects of years of radiation exposure, the dreaded spacers.

———

I was on the bridge for docking. I was actually on the bridge for docking. Daddy had let me come onto the bridge for docking.

Benji was in the co-pilot's seat, strapped in with only four points. Ramon was in the sensor operator's seat, also strapped in with only four points. Daddy was in the pilot's chair, strapped in with only four points. But I was in the rarely used navigator's chair, strapped in with all five points. I didn't have anything special I had to do, just watch.

My sensors helmet was plugged in, and I could slip it on when I wanted to, but right now I was watching the gauges with Benji.

"Captain, we're showing 15,000 meters per second and slowing." Benji was trying to sound extra professional, but his voice kept cracking. "Range to Marsport is 250,000 meters."

Daddy got on comms. "MECO in 15 seconds." Then he looked around. "Everyone buckled in?"

"Yes, Daddy," I replied.

"Yes, Captain," Benji said with another one of those voice squeaks that were becoming too common for him.

"Yes, Jason," Ramon replied, but his voice was muffled by his helmet.

"MECO in 5…4…3…2…1…MARK!"

I slipped on the sensors helmet just as the ship went into zero-g. I knew, down in engineering, that Mommy had just turned off the engines, and there would be a bunch of work she would be doing with Jax and Pete to secure the reactors. Krissy would be interested, but I liked the bridge.

"What is our speed and range?"

"We're at 747 meters per second constant, 75,000 meters, and closing."

"Marsport, Bartlett Family on final. Please confirm."

"Bartlett Family, you are clear for Dock 17. Atmospheric unload and airlock connection confirmed."

"Thank you, Marsport."

"Benji, do you see the dock lights for our dock?"

"I see them, Daddy." I could see them in the sensors. They were really obvious from the ship's sensors."

"I have them, Captain."

"Do we need to make a course correction?"

"A touch starboard up, I think?"

"Good eye."

The ship moved a tiny bit. I could tell more because I had the sensors helmet on.

"There is a ship coming across our bow," I warned.

"Confirmed," Ramon echoed.

"Unknown ship, Bartlett family is on an unpowered dock approach."

The other ship's maneuvering jets fired. I could see a lot of helium dumping into space, and they moved out of our way. We passed under them by a few meters.

"That was close," Ramon said.

"I felt them pass," I commented. I could, too. They brushed my whiskers, or so it felt.

"Marsport, please identify unknown traffic?"

"Bartlett Family, unknown traffic is unknown. Port is investigating."

Using the sensors helmet, I watched the ship drift into the dock, and the docking clamps grabbed us.

"Ship docked and secure," Daddy announced. "Prepare for cargo operations."

I slipped off my helmet and looked at Daddy. "We're here."

"We're at Mars, Danno. We made it. King is going to go back to Earth. We're going to Ceres. Mommy is going to have a new baby kit. Benji is going to be my official co-pilot, and we're still flying."

My tail started wagging so hard I started spinning. "And I'm going to be a junior sensors operator."

"Yes, you are. And you are going to be a big help."

ABOUT THE AUTHOR

Randall Fox is the pseudonym Ron Oakes uses when writing novellas about Randall and his friends.

Ron Oakes is a computer scientist, science fiction and fantasy fan, and self-published fantasy writer based in Albuquerque, New Mexico. Some of his earliest memories include watching *Star Trek* on weekday afternoons and desiring to work on computers like those found on the U.S.S. Enterprise. Not long afterward, he saw *Star Wars* in its original incarnation (before it became *Episode IV: A New Hope*).

In the late 1970s, through his Boy Scouts troop, he was introduced to Dungeons & Dragons. At around the same time, he was introduced to the *Chronicles of Prydain* by Lloyd Alexander. These combined to create a love of fantasy.

After college, he moved to the Chicago Suburbs. His love of D&D and other tabletop role-playing games led him to discover organized Science Fiction Fandom in the early 1990s. As a fan and convention runner, he has worked on and run conventions in Chicago, San Diego, and Albuquerque.

He is married to another fan and works as a government contractor in Albuquerque. He shares his house with his wife, four cats, over 300 robots, multiple lightsabers, more artwork than the walls can hold, several dragons, and assorted stuffed animals—not all of which are from this world.

ALSO BY RANDALL FOX

UNITED CREATURES UNIVERE STORIES

Freight, Family and Fire

Half-Tonne of Silence

Trial and Consequences

RANDALL FOX STORIES

Flight of the Heretics

The Prey's Rebellion

The Wolf and The Parliament

The Hermitage and The Henge

The Tunnel and The Ox

The Duchess and The Fox

The Cougar and The Quest

The Books and The Guardian

The Kitsune and The Kit

The Transformation and The Future

The Pup and The Adventure

The Moose and The Crown

The Stoat and The Pilgrims

The Muzzle and The Pursuit

The Potion and The Madness

The Priest and The Gang

The Lord and The Fires

The Wolf and The Champion

The Bear and The Squirrel

The Reindeer and the Stone Circle

The Catacombs and The Wolf

The Friends and The Walk

The Trickster and The Cabin

The Fox and The Letter

The Mouse and The Squirrels

The Executor and The Revenge

INSPECTOR BEAUREGARD STORIES

The Inspector and The Robber

The Inspector and The Magistrate

The Inspector And His Son

The Advocate and The Duke

———

AS RON OAKES

The Phoenix Knives

www.ingramcontent.com/pod-product-compliance
Lightning Source LLC
Chambersburg PA
CBHW051547050726
47595CB00002B/671